"Miss Kemp already wrote this year's assignment on the board," I told Imogene, "and it isn't a science project."

"Fine time to tell me," Imogene grunted. "What is it? The assignment." She shook the oatmeal box she was holding. "Is it mice?"

"No," I said, "it's about people."

"Mice would be better," Imogene said.

Later that morning Miss Kemp explained her assignment, and I thought Imogene might be right.

OTHER BOOKS BY BARBARA ROBINSON

The Best Christmas Pageant Ever

The Best Halloween Ever

My Brother Louis Measures Worms
And Other Louis Stories

Barbara Robinson

The ~~Worst~~ Best School Year Ever

HarperTrophy®
An Imprint of HarperCollins*Publishers*

Harper Trophy® is a registered trademark of
HarperCollins Publishers Inc.

The Best School Year Ever
Copyright © 1994 by Barbara Robinson
Library of Congress Cataloging-in-Publication Data
Robinson, Barbara.
The best school year ever / Barbara Robinson.
    p.   cm.
Sequel to: The best Christmas pageant ever.
Summary: The six horrible Herdmans, the worst kids in
the history of the world, cause mayhem throughout the
school year.
    ISBN 0-06-023039-8 — ISBN 0-06-023043-6 (lib. bdg.)
ISBN 0-06-440492-7 (pbk.)
    [1. Schools—Fiction. 2. Humorous stories.] I. Title.
PZ7.R5628Bg 1994   93-50891
[Fic]—dc20   CIP
                                                                      AC

❖

First Harper Trophy edition, 1997
Revised Harper Trophy edition, 2005
Visit us on the World Wide Web!
www.harperchildrens.com

11 12 13 LP/CW 50 49 48 47 46 45

This book is for my daughters—
Carolyn and Margie,
who brighten all the corners of my life. . . .
—B.R.

The Best ~~Worst~~ School Year Ever

THE HERDMANS...
BACK AGAIN!

When we studied the Old West, everybody had to do a special report on A Cowboy's Life or Famous Indian Chiefs or Notorious Outlaw Families like the James brothers. Boomer Malone picked the James brothers, but then he couldn't find them in the children's encyclopedia.

"That's all right, Boomer," Miss Kemp said. "It doesn't have to be the James brothers. Pick another outlaw family."

So Boomer did. He picked the Herdmans.

Of course, the Herdmans weren't in the Old West, and they weren't in the children's encyclopedia either. They were right there in the Woodrow Wilson School, all six of them spread out, one to a class, because the only teacher who could put up with two of them at once would have to be a Miss King Kong.

My father said he bet that was in the teachers' contracts along with sick leave and medical benefits: only one Herdman at a time.

Boomer's paper was the best one, three whole pages of one crime after another. He should have gotten A plus, but Miss Kemp made him do the whole paper over.

"I'm ashamed of you, Boomer," she said, "calling your own schoolmates an outlaw family."

The Herdmans didn't care. They knew they were outlaws. So did Miss Kemp, but I guess she had to pretend they were like everybody else.

They weren't, and if they *had* been around in the Old West, they would have burned it all down or blown it all up and we wouldn't have to study about it.

Plus, of course, we wouldn't have to live with Herdmans every day, in school and out. . . .

1

Unless you're somebody like Huckleberry Finn, the first day of school isn't too bad. Most kids, by then, are bored with summer and itchy from mosquito bites and poison ivy and nothing to do. Your sneakers are all worn out and you can't get new ones till school starts and your mother is sick and tired of yelling at you to pick things up and you're sick and tired of picking the same things up.

Plus, the first day of school is only half a day for kids.

My little brother, Charlie, once asked my mother what the teachers do for the rest of the day.

"They get things ready—books and papers and lessons."

"That's not what Leroy Herdman says," Charlie told her. "Leroy says as soon as the kids are gone, they lock all the doors and order in pizza and beer."

"Well, they don't," Mother said, "and how would Leroy know anyway?"

"He forgot something," Charlie said, "and he went back to get it and he couldn't get in."

"They saw him coming and locked the doors," Mother said. "Wouldn't you?"

Well, yes. Anyone would, because the Herdmans—Ralph, Imogene, Leroy, Claude, Ollie, and Gladys—were the worst kids in the history of the world. They weren't honest or cheerful or industrious or cooperative or clean.

They told lies and smoked cigars and set fire to things and hit little kids and cursed and stayed away from school whenever they wanted to and wouldn't learn anything when they were there.

They were always there, though, on the first day, so you always knew right away that this was going to be another exciting Herdman year in the Woodrow Wilson Elementary School.

At least there was only one of them in each grade, and since they never got kept back, you always had the same one to put up with. I had Imogene, and what I did was stay out of her way, but it wasn't easy.

This time she grabbed me in the hall and shoved an oatmeal box in my face. "Hey," she said, "you want to buy a science project?"

I figured that Imogene's idea of a science project would probably explode or catch fire or smell really bad or be alive and bite me— and, in fact, I could hear something squealing and scratching around in the oatmeal box.

"Miss Kemp already wrote this year's assignment on the board," I said, "and it isn't a science project."

"Fine time to tell me," Imogene grunted. "What is it? The assignment." She shook her oatmeal box. "Is it mice?"

So I was half right—Imogene's science project was alive, but it probably wouldn't bite me unless it was great big mice, and I didn't want to find out.

"No," I said, "it's about people."

"Mice would be better," Imogene said.

Later that morning Miss Kemp explained her assignment, and I thought Imogene might be right, because the assignment sounded weird.

"For this year's project," she said, "we're going to study each other. That's the assignment on the blackboard, Compliments for Classmates."

All over the room hands were going up and kids were saying "Huh?" and "What does it mean?" and "How many pages?" But Miss Kemp ignored all this.

"It means exactly what it says," she said. "You're to think of a special compliment for each person in this class, and please don't groan"—a lot of people did anyway— "because this is the assignment for the *year*. You have all year to think about it, and next June, before the last day of school, you'll draw names from a hat and think of more compliments for just that one person."

Somebody asked if it could be a famous person instead, and somebody else asked if it could be a dead famous person, like George Washington.

Miss Kemp said no. "This is a classroom project, so it has to be people in this class. We know all about George Washington's good points, but . . ." She looked around and picked on Boomer. "We don't know all Boomer's good points. More important, *Boomer* probably doesn't know all his good points."

"How many compliments?" Junior Jacobs wanted to know.

"Up to you," Miss Kemp said.

Alice Wendleken raised her hand. "Would beautiful hair and shiny hair count as one compliment?"

This sounded to me as if Alice planned to compliment herself, which would save someone else the trouble, but Miss Kemp said, "I'm not talking about beautiful hair and nice teeth, Alice. I mean characteristics, personal qualities, something special."

This could be hard, I thought. Take Albert Pelfrey. When you think of Albert Pelfrey, you think *fat*. Even Albert thinks *fat*. It's hard to think anything else, so I would really have to study Albert to find some special personal quality that wasn't just about being fat. And besides Albert there were twenty-eight other people, including Imogene Herdman.

"What's a compliment?" Imogene asked me.

"It's something nice you tell someone, like if someone is especially helpful or especially friendly."

Alice looked Imogene up and down. "Or especially clean," she said.

"Okay." Imogene frowned. "But mice would still be better."

Mice would probably be *easier* for Imogene because the Herdmans always had animals around. As far as I know they weren't mean to the animals, but the animals they weren't mean to were mean all by themselves, like their cat, which was crazy and had to be kept on a chain because it bit people.

Now and then you would see Mrs.

Herdman walking the cat around the block on its chain, but she worked two shifts at the shoe factory and didn't have much time left over to hang around the house and walk the cat.

There wasn't any Mr. Herdman. Everybody agreed that after Gladys was born, he just climbed on a freight train and left town, but some people said he did it right away and some people said he waited a year or two.

"Gladys probably bit him," my friend Alice Wendleken said.

"Not if she was a baby?" I asked. "Babies don't have any teeth."

"She probably had hard, hard gums." Alice knew what she was talking about, because Gladys bit her all the time. Mrs. Wendleken always poured iodine all over the bites, so Alice had to go around for days with big brown splotches on her arms and legs. Alice was always afraid she would die anyway (of Gladys-bite) and have to be buried looking splotched up and ugly instead of beautiful in her blue-and-white dress with the ruffles.

It wasn't all that special to get bitten by Gladys. She bit everybody, including my little brother, Charlie. Charlie came home yelling and screaming that Gladys bit him, and Gladys came too, which shows you how fearless they were. Any other kid who bit a kid and broke the skin and drew blood would go hide somewhere, but not Gladys.

"Gladys Herdman!" It's always your whole name when my mother is mad. "Do you know what I think about a little girl who bites people? I think she ought to have to wear a sign around her neck that says 'Beware of Gladys.'"

I guess Mother thought that would really put Gladys in her place, but Gladys just said "Okay" and went home and made the sign and wore it for a week. Nobody paid much attention—we didn't need a sign to make us beware of Gladys.

Besides everything else they did, the Herdmans would steal anything they could carry, and it was surprising what all they could carry—not just candy and gum and gerbils and goldfish. They even stole Mrs. Johanneson's concrete birdbath, for the goldfish, I guess. And last spring they stole my friend Louella McCluskey's baby brother, Howard, from in front of the grocery store.

Of course Howard wasn't supposed to be in front of the grocery store. Louella was supposed to be baby-sitting him, which she did every Tuesday afternoon while her mother went to the beauty parlor. Louella got paid fifty cents to do this, and on that particular Tuesday we were in the grocery store spending her fifty cents.

When we came out—no Howard. The stroller was still there, though, and that's why we didn't think of the Herdmans right away. Usually if you missed something, you would just naturally figure the Herdmans had it. But when they stole a thing, they always stole all of the thing. It wasn't like them to take the baby and leave the stroller.

Louella turned the stroller over and looked underneath it as if she thought Howard might have fallen through, which was pretty dumb. Then we walked up and down the street, hollering for Howard, which was also dumb. How could Howard answer? He couldn't even talk. He couldn't walk either, or crawl very much. He couldn't get out of the stroller in the first place.

"Well, somebody must have taken him," Louella said. "Some stranger has just walked off with my baby brother."

"You better tell a policeman," I said.

"No, I don't want to. They would get my mother out of the beauty parlor and I don't want her to know."

"She'll know when you come home without Howard," I said.

"I won't go home. Not till I find him. Now let's just think. Who would take Howard?"

I couldn't imagine who would take Howard. Even my mother said Howard was the homeliest baby she'd ever laid eyes on, but she did say that he would probably be just fine once he grew some hair. That was his main trouble—having no hair. Here he was, bald as an egg, and Mrs. McCluskey kept rubbing his head with Vaseline to make the hair grow. So when you looked at Howard, all you saw was this shiny white head. Not too good.

"Probably someone who just loves babies," Louella said, but that could be anybody. It would be easier to think of someone who hates babies, but if you hated them you certainly wouldn't steal one.

Then Louella had another idea. "Let's just walk down the street," she said, "pushing the stroller. Maybe someone has seen Howard and when they see us with an empty stroller they'll figure we're looking for him and tell us where he is."

I was pretty disgusted. "Louella," I said, "you know that won't happen."

But it did. The first person we met was my little brother, Charlie, and the first thing he said was "If you're looking for Howard, the Herdmans have got him."

Louella looked relieved, but not very, and I didn't blame her. If you had to choose between a total stranger having your baby brother and the Herdmans having him, you would pick the total stranger every time.

"What have they done with him?" Louella asked.

"They're charging kids a quarter to look at him."

"Why would anybody pay a quarter to look at Howard?" I said. "We can look at Howard anytime."

"They don't tell you it's Howard. They've got a sign up that says, 'See the Amazing Tattooed Baby! 25 cents.'"

"They tattooed him!" Louella yelped. "My mother will kill me!"

Actually, they didn't tattoo him. What they did was wipe off the Vaseline and draw pictures all over his head with waterproof marker.

Charlie was dumb enough to fall for their sign. He paid his quarter to see an amazing tattooed baby, and of course he was mad as could be when it turned out to be Howard McCluskey with pictures drawn all over his head.

So he tagged along behind us, insisting that Louella get his money back, but we both knew that Louella would have all she could do just to get Howard back.

"If it was anything but the baby," she said, "I wouldn't even *try* to get it back—not from the Herdmans."

"They already collected six-fifty," Charlie said. "You ought to make them pay you some of that for the use of Howard."

"I'll probably have to pay them," Louella grumbled.

She was right. When we got to the Herdmans', there were three or four kids lined up outside the fence, and Louella marched up and said to Imogene Herdman, "You give me back my baby brother!"

But Imogene pretended not to hear her and just went on collecting money. "You want to see the tattooed baby?" She jiggled the money box at Louella. "It'll cost you a quarter."

"It's no tattooed baby," Louella said, "It's my little brother."

Imogene squinched her eyes together. "How do you know?"

"I just know."

"You do not. It could be anybody's baby. It could be some baby you never heard of. It'll cost you a quarter to find out."

Sure enough, it was Howard and he was a sight. The whole top of his head was red and green and blue and purple with pictures of dogs and cats and trees and tic-tac-toe games.

"I don't know what you're so mad about," Leroy Herdman said. "He looks a lot better than he did."

In a way Leroy was right. Howard looked a lot more *interesting*, but nobody expected Mrs. McCluskey to think so.

We took Howard out back of my house and tried to wash off his head, which is how we found out the pictures were all waterproof.

"Now what'll I do?" Louella asked.

"Tell your mother the Herdmans did it," Charlie said.

"She'll just want to know why I let them do it, and how they got hold of him in the first place. Maybe we should use some soap."

We tried all kinds of things on Howard, but the only thing that worked at all was scouring powder, and that didn't work too well. It made his head gritty and it didn't take off all the purple.

"If you don't stand too close to him," Louella said, "and then squint your eyes . . . does the purple look to you like veins?"

It didn't to me. "But after all," I told Louella, "I *know* what it is. Your mother doesn't know what it is, so maybe it will look like veins to her."

It didn't. Mrs. McCluskey was so mad that she got a sick headache and spots before her eyes and had to lie down for two days. The first thing she did after she got up was go to work on Howard's head to try and get the purple off, and she discovered two or three patches of soft fuzz.

So then she wasn't mad at the Herdmans anymore. She said that something about all the drawing or the Magic Marker ink must have started his hair to grow. But she was still mad at Louella, which didn't seem fair. After all, it *could* have been the scouring powder.

I said that to my mother, and I knew right away that it was a mistake, because she said, "What scouring powder?" and then, "Beth Bradley, come back here! What scouring powder?"

So then I got punished for putting scouring powder on Howard's head, and Louella got punished for leaving him in front of the grocery store, and Charlie got punished by not having any Choco-Whoopee bars from the ice cream man till next week.

"That's what your quarter was for,"

Mother told him. "Next time you'll think twice before you throw away your quarter on something silly."

Of course, Howard got some hair, but he was just a baby and he didn't care whether he had any hair or not. The Herdmans, who caused all the trouble in the first place, got $6.50.

If anybody but the Herdmans had stolen a baby and scribbled all over his head and then charged people money to look at him, they would have been shut up in the house for the rest of their natural lives. But since it *was* the Herdmans, most people just said how lucky Mrs. McCluskey was to get Howard back all in one piece, and that was that.

The truth is that no one wanted to fool around with them, so you knew that unless they tried to hold up the First National Bank or burn down the public library, you weren't going to see the last of them—especially if you had to go to the Woodrow Wilson School, and be in the same class with Imogene, and figure out something good to say about her before the end of the year.

2

A lot of people, like Alice Wendleken's mother, thought the Herdmans ought to be in jail, kids or not, but I knew that wouldn't happen.

Our jail is just two cells in the basement of the town hall, and the Herdmans aren't allowed in the town hall anymore since Gladys and Ollie put all the frogs in the drinking fountain there. They were little tiny frogs, and Miss Farley, the town clerk, drank two or three of them off the top of the bubbler by mistake.

She didn't have her glasses on, she said, and didn't see them till somebody hollered, "Evelyn, stop! You're drinking frogs!"

Miss Farley was hysterical! She said she could feel them jerking and jumping all up and down her windpipe. But even so she chased Gladys and Ollie all around the block, and she said if she ever caught any Herdmans inside the town hall again, she would put on roller skates and run them out of town so fast their heels would smoke.

Of course they didn't care. "What'd she eat our frogs for anyway?" Gladys said. "It's not our fault she ate our frogs. She'll get warts in her stomach, where she can't scratch them."

"Warts don't itch," Alice Wendleken told her.

"These will," Gladys said. "We caught the frogs in a patch of poison ivy."

The town hall wasn't the only place in

town where the Herdmans weren't allowed in to get a drink of water or go to the bathroom or call their mother or anything. They also weren't allowed in the drugstore or the movie theater or the A&P or the Tasti-Lunch Diner.

They used to be allowed in the post office, but that didn't last. Somebody got hold of all their school pictures and put them up right next to the "WANTED" posters, and it seemed so natural for them to be there that nobody noticed till Ollie Herdman went up and asked the postmaster, Mr. Blair, how much money he could get for his brother Claude.

"I don't know what you mean," Mr. Blair said.

"Some of those people are worth five hundred dollars," Ollie said. "How much can I get for Claude?"

So Mr. Blair went to see what he was talking about and sure enough, there were the Herdmans right up with the bank robbers and the mad bombers and all.

Mr. Blair had a fit. "How did these pictures get up here?" he said: "Did you put these pictures up here?"

Ollie said no, it was a big surprise to him.

"Well, it's a big surprise to me too," Mr. Blair said, "but I can tell you that the F.B.I. is not going to pay you anything for Claude, or any of the rest of you either. How did you happen to pick on Claude?"

"Because he's the one I've got," Ollie said.

Mr. Blair said later that he didn't like the sound of that. "I figured he probably had Claude tied to a tree somewhere." So he mentioned it to the policeman on the corner, and the policeman said he'd better go investigate because with Herdmans you never could tell.

He didn't have to go far. There was a big crowd of people and a lot of commotion halfway down the block, and sure enough, Ollie had shut Claude up in the men's room of the Sunoco station.

When the policeman got there, Claude was banging on the door and hollering for someone to let him out, and there was a whole big family from South Dakota wanting to get in. The mother said they had driven almost a hundred and fifty miles looking for a Sunoco station because they were the cleanest, but what good was clean if you couldn't get in?

"I gave the key to one of those Herdmans," the manager said, "and he went off with it. I should have my head examined."

"But you don't need a key to get out," the policeman said. "Why doesn't Claude just open the door?"

"I can't," Claude yelled. "The door's stuck."

Ollie claimed later that he didn't have

anything to do with that; that he hadn't even planned to shut Claude up in the men's room or anywhere else, but when the door jammed shut he went off to get help, and that was when he saw the pictures at the post office.

"You were going to get help at the post office?" the manager asked.

"I was going to get my sister Imogene."

"And she was at the post office?"

"No," Ollie said, "she wasn't there."

That was typical Herdman—there was a lie in it somewhere, but you couldn't put your finger on where.

Of course all that was later. In the meantime Mr. Blair and the Sunoco station manager had to get the fire department to break in the door and get Claude out. By that time the South Dakota people had left, and a lot of other people who wanted gas got tired of waiting and went somewhere else, and in all the excitement somebody walked off with two cans of motor oil and a wrench. Herdmans, probably, but nobody could prove it, just like nobody could prove that Ollie really meant to hand Claude over to the F.B.I. for money.

So then the Herdmans weren't allowed in the post office *or* the Sunoco station, and they got thrown out of the new Laundromat the very day it opened.

They planned to wash their cat in one of the machines, but they didn't know it would cost money, so they just dropped him in and went off to locate some quarters.

Of course the cat didn't like it in the washing machine, and it made so much noise hissing and spitting and scratching that the manager, Mr. Cleveland, went to see what was wrong.

"I thought it was a short circuit," he said, "or a loose connection—something electrical. That's the kind of noise it was."

People said it *looked* electrical, all right. When he opened the lid, the cat shot out with its tail and its ears and all its hair standing straight up. It skittered around all over the tops of the machines and clawed through everybody's laundry baskets, and knocked over boxes of soap and bottles of bleach and a big basket of flowers that said "Good Luck to the Laundromat."

Finally someone opened the door, and the last they saw of the cat it was roaring down the street, all tangled up in a tablecloth.

Of course the Laundromat was a mess and all the customers were mad and couldn't find their clothes and wanted their money back for the stuff the cat had spilled. Pretty soon people began to sneeze from all the cat hair and soap powder in the air, and one lady broke out in big red blotches all over because she was allergic to cats. Mr. Cleveland sent everyone outdoors till things settled down.

But things didn't settle down. Santoro's Pizza Parlor was across the street, and when Mr. Santoro saw all these people coming out of the Laundromat sneezing and coughing and choking, he yelled, "What's the matter? Is it a fire?"

Somebody yelled back, "No—cat hair." But Mr. Santoro thought they said "bad air." He figured there was something wrong with the new plumbing connections, maybe a gas leak, and he ran to the top of the street to warn people away in case of an explosion.

Some of the people he warned away were Herdmans—Imogene and Ralph and Leroy, on their way back with fifty cents for the washing machine.

"You children get away from here!" he said. "The Laundromat may explode!"

I guess they were pretty surprised. They probably figured the cat did it, but they didn't know how. They also probably figured that if the cat was smart enough to blow up a Laundromat, it was smart enough to get away. So they just left.

Mr. Santoro called the fire department too and they came right away. But of course there wasn't any fire and there wasn't any gas leak, and by that time there wasn't any cat and there weren't any Herdmans either, just a lot of angry customers and a reporter from the newspaper who went around interviewing everybody.

Most of the people didn't even know what had happened because it happened so fast, so the newspaper story was pretty mysterious. "LAUNDROMAT OPENING MARRED BY UNUSUAL DISTURBANCE," it said. "FIREMEN RESPOND TO ANONYMOUS ALARM. CUSTOMERS DESCRIBE WILD ANIMAL." My father said at least they got that part right.

Mr. Cleveland had to clean up the mess and replace everybody's stuff and pay for the blotched-up lady to get an allergy shot, so he was pretty mad. Mr. Santoro was mad because they called him "anonymous," and of course the firemen were mad because they knew the Herdmans did it, whatever it was.

In the meantime the Herdmans were home, waiting for the cat to show up. The cat, crazier than usual because it was all wrapped up in a tablecloth, was tearing all over town, yowling and spitting and scratching at anything that got in its way.

It ran in the barber shop and streaked up one side of the chair where Mr. Perry was shaving someone.

"All of a sudden," Mr. Perry said, "there was a cat. So I lathered the cat by mistake. Missed my customer and lathered the cat."

Then the cat ran through the lobby of the movie theater and picked up some popcorn there, and by that time you couldn't tell what it was or what it had *ever* been.

It finally clawed its way up a tree in front of the library, and the librarian, Miss Graebner, called the fire department to come and get it down.

"I think it's a cat," she said, "and it looks like it's been through a war."

"No," the fire chief said, "it's been through a washing machine, and as far as I'm concerned it can stay in that tree till the middle of next year." Of course, Miss Graebner was mad about that.

The only people who weren't mad were the Herdmans, because when the cat finally came home, it was all clean and fluffy from the shaving lather, and that's what they wanted in the first place.

3

*N*aturally my mother wasn't too crazy about the Herdmans since they were always mopping up the floor with Charlie, but she had too much to do, she said, to spend time complaining about them—she would leave that to Alice Wendleken's mother, who was so good at it.

Mrs. Wendleken complained about them all the time, to everybody. It was her second favorite subject, besides how smart Alice was, and how pretty, and how talented, and how it would all go to waste if Gladys Herdman bit her to death.

Every time you turned around, Mrs. Wendleken was volunteering Alice to be the star of something—the main fairy or the head elf or the Clean Up Our Streets poster girl— and when the Chamber of Commerce bought a respirator for the hospital they put a picture of it in the paper and, sure enough, there was Alice hooked up to the respirator.

Mrs. Wendleken said she didn't have anything to do with that. The photographer just looked around and said, "I wonder if that pretty little girl would be willing to pose with the respirator." But nobody believed her.

Alice didn't get any applause for this either, but she carried the picture around anyway, and showed it to anyone who would hold still. She showed it to Imogene Herdman at recess, and Imogene took one look and hollered, "Get away from me! Don't touch

me! Whatever you've got, I don't want it!"—
which brought the school nurse in a hurry in
case Alice had smallpox or something.

It emptied the playground in a hurry too.
Everybody figured that if it was something
Imogene Herdman was scared to catch, it
would wipe out the rest of us because ordinary
germs didn't even slow the Herdmans down.
They never got mumps or pinkeye or colds or
stomachaches or anything. A snake once bit
Leroy Herdman and Leroy's leg swelled up a
little bit, but that was all.

The snake died. Leroy brought it to
school and tied it all up and down the light
cord in the teachers' supply closet, and about
five minutes later the kindergarten teacher,
Miss Newman, came in and pulled the cord.

She had all the day's helpers with her—six
kindergarten kids carrying pots of red finger
paint—and when Miss Newman screamed,
they all dropped their pots and finger paint

flew all over the place.

Then somebody upset two big boxes of chalk and they all tramped around in that, and when the janitor heard the racket and opened the door, he just took one look and went straight to get the principal. He said there had been some terrible accident and the supply closet was full of bloody people, apparently all cut up and screaming in pain.

By the time the principal got there, Miss Newman had pulled herself together and was herding the little kids down the hall to the washroom, and then the recess bell rang.

So the hall was full of kids, and teachers calling to Miss Newman, "What happened? What happened?" and the principal telling everyone to "Move along, move right along. Nothing here to see." Of course there was plenty to see—the whole thing looked like a big disaster we had just read about in history called The Children's Massacre.

In all the commotion Leroy Herdman just walked into the supply closet, untied his snake and put it in his pocket, and walked out again.

When we got back from recess, the principal and Miss Newman and the janitor and the boys' basketball coach were all crawling around the floor of the supply closet, and Miss Newman was saying, "I tell you there was a snake crawling up the light cord!"

Of course they never did find it, because nobody looked in Leroy's pocket.

I couldn't understand why the snake died and Leroy didn't, but when I asked my father, he said that Leroy probably stretched his story. "A snake bit him," my father said, "and then he found a different snake that was already dead. That's what I think."

My mother said she bet it wasn't a snake at all, that Leroy just tied a whole lot of poor worms together. But I decided that Leroy was telling the truth for the first time in his life, that the snake was perfectly healthy, bit Leroy, and immediately died. So maybe Mrs. Wendleken wasn't far wrong to pour iodine all over Alice, and maybe Alice should shut up about this treatment and just be glad she wasn't dead, like the snake.

Two or three days later Leroy stuck the snake in the third-grade pencil sharpener, tail first, and that teacher went all to pieces too. It was bad enough, she said, to find a snake in the pencil sharpener, but then she almost sharpened it by mistake.

The snake was pretty worn out by then, so they threw it away, but nobody in the third grade would go near the pencil sharpener for the rest of the week.

My mother's friend Miss Philips worked for the welfare department, and one of her jobs was to check up on the Herdmans, so Mother told her about the snakebite in case

Leroy should get some kind of shot for it. But Miss Philips just said she didn't know of any shot that would benefit Leroy, and anyway, all her sympathies were with the snake.

"I went once to that garage where those kids live," she said, "but I never got inside and I barely got out of the yard alive. It was full of rocks and poison ivy and torn-up bicycles and pieces of cars and great big holes they'd dug. I fell in one of the holes and the cat jumped on me out of a window. Good thing I had a hat on or I'd be bald. Now I just drive past the place once a month, and if they haven't managed to blow it up or burn it down, I figure they're all right."

"But a snakebite," Mother said. "Don't you think that's unusual?"

"I certainly do," Miss Philips said. "It's the first time something bit one of them instead of the other way around."

The whole thing got into the newspaper:

"REPTILE FOUND IN WOODROW WILSON SCHOOL," the article said. "TEACHERS AND STUDENTS ALARMED." That probably meant Miss Newman and all the kindergarten kids. "PARENTS SEEK ACTION" probably meant Mrs. Wendleken, seeking to get the Herdmans expelled or arrested or something. "SCHOOL OFFICIAL INSPECTS PREMISES" *was* Mr. Crabtree, the principal, who stuck his head in the third-grade room and said that if one more snake showed up anywhere he would personally kill it, skin it, cook it, and feed it to whoever was responsible.

I don't know whether that would have scared Leroy or not, but it didn't matter anyway because he wasn't there. Imogene said he stayed home to bury the snake, and she had this messy scribbled-up note that said, "Leroy is absent at a funeral."

"I'm sorry to hear that, Imogene," the teacher said. "Was it a member of your family?

Why aren't you at the funeral?"

"It was a friend of Leroy's," Imogene said. "I didn't like him."

Mrs. Wendleken was mad because the newspaper article didn't say it was Leroy Herdman's snake that caused all this trouble, and she was mad at the principal because he wouldn't say so either.

"I can't *prove* who the snake belonged to," Mr. Crabtree said, "and even if I could, why would I? It wasn't a boa constrictor, you know, and it was dead to begin with."

But I guess Mrs. Wendleken was really out to nail Leroy, and she wouldn't give up. "Of course it was Leroy's snake! Everybody knows it was Leroy's snake. Why else would he bury it? Why would Leroy Herdman bury someone else's snake?"

"I don't know." Mr. Crabtree was fed up with the snake and Leroy Herdman and Mrs. Wendleken too. "But if he *did* bury a snake for somebody else, it's the first cooperative thing he's ever done in his life, and I just think we ought to drop the whole subject, don't you?"

That would probably have been the end of it, except that Mrs. Wendleken described this conversation to my mother, who described it to Miss Philips. Then Miss Philips went to school and told Mr. Crabtree that she had a plan to civilize the Herdmans or, at least, one of them.

"It's about the snake . . ." she began, but Mr. Crabtree wouldn't let her say any more.

"I'll do it," he said. "I don't even care what it is you want, just so I don't have to hear any more about that snake."

So Leroy got named Good School Citizen of the Month—"for an act of kindness," the award read.

Of course this was one big surprise to everybody, especially Leroy, and it nearly killed Alice Wendleken, who had piled up more good deeds and good grades and extra-credit projects and perfect-attendance records than anybody else in the whole history of the Woodrow Wilson School, and expected to be the Good School Citizen of the Month for the rest of her life.

Nobody could figure out what kind thing Leroy had done, but Miss Philips told my mother.

"He buried a snake?" Mother said. "That's it?"

"That's it," Miss Philips said.

"Well, I guess if you were the snake you might call it an act of kindness, but I don't understand . . ."

"I just thought he might decide to live up to the honor," Miss Philips explained. "He might be a changed person."

Mother said she wouldn't count on it. "He probably doesn't even know what it was he did."

"He didn't even do it," Charlie told her. "Imogene just said he did. Nobody buried the snake. The janitor threw it in the trash masher. I saw him."

"Well, don't tell anyone," Mother said. "Mrs. Wendleken would never shut up about it."

Mother was right about Leroy. He *didn't* know what he did or how he got to be a Good School Citizen, and when Charlie wouldn't tell him, he buried Charlie up to his neck in the trash masher barrel, which would have been tough on Charlie if the janitor didn't happen to see him before he mashed up the trash.

So Leroy wasn't a changed person, unless you want to count that he only buried Charlie up to his neck instead of all the way.

4

The janitor, Mr. Sprague, said that was that—no more trash masher. He told the principal that we could have a trash masher or we could have the Herdmans, but we couldn't have both under one roof.

"I can't stand around and guard the thing all day," he said. "There's six of them and only one of me, and every time I leave the basement to go sweep a floor, they shove something else into it."

They'd already mashed up the fourth-grade

ant farm and the plastic dinosaur exhibit, and then Leroy went ahead and mashed up the Good School Citizen Award too, once he found out he couldn't eat it or spend it or sell it to anybody.

Alice reported this to her mother, and Mrs. Wendleken was so disgusted about the whole thing that she resigned from the PTA, which my father said was good news for the PTA.

Of course, Mrs. Wendleken didn't come right out and say, "I quit because I'm mad at everybody." She just said it wasn't fair for her to run the PTA Talent Show because Alice was in it. She said Mother could do that because Mother *didn't* have any talented children in it.

"Does that mean we aren't talented, or just that we aren't in it?" Charlie asked me, and I said, "Both."

Actually *nobody* had any talented children

in it, and they really had to scratch around to get kids to do anything, so it was no night of a thousand stars, which was what all the posters said—"Night of a Thousand Stars! An Evening of Family Entertainment! PTA Talent Show!"

When my father saw the list of acts, he said he hoped there would be more talent in the refreshments than there was going to be in the show.

"There aren't any refreshments," Mother told him. "This is just an evening of family entertainment."

He shook his head. "Not unless you have refreshments, it won't be."

I guess Mother took another look at the list, because that night she called around for people to make cookies and brownies and cupcakes and punch, and the next day the posters said, "Night of a Thousand Stars! An Evening of Family Entertainment! PTA Talent

Show!"—with "Delicious Refreshments!" crowded in at the bottom.

This was a big mistake, because "refreshments" is one long word that all the Herdmans understand, and right away you knew that they'd figure some way to get at them.

"They can't," Alice said. "They'd have to be in the show, and they can't do anything talented."

"They can steal," Charlie said.

Alice looked at him the way my mother looks at the bottom of the hamster cage. "That's not a talent," she said.

Maybe not, but the Herdmans did it better than anybody else. Still, it was hard to see how they would do it for an audience or what they would call it on the program or what they would steal, because there wasn't much left that they hadn't already stolen.

Last year they were all absent on October 4 and we had Arbor Day because for the last three years the Herdmans stole the tree, and the principal said at least this year we'd finally get it planted, even if it died over the winter.

"Maybe they've got some talent we don't know about," I said. And sure enough, three days later Gladys Herdman took a pair of kindergarten safety scissors and cut Eugene Preston's hair in the shape of a dog. It could have been a cat, though, or a horse or a pig. Something with four legs and a tail, anyway, or else something with five legs and no tail.

You had to look right down at the top of his head to see it, but this was what you mostly saw of Eugene anyway because he was the shortest kid in the second grade or the first grade or even kindergarten. So naturally he got picked on a lot, and if you had to choose which kid in the Woodrow Wilson School would get his hair cut in the shape of a dog for no reason, you would choose Eugene.

Of course he was already a nervous wreck from being the shortest kid around, and you knew it wasn't going to calm him down to have people holler, "Here, Fido!" or "Here, Spot!" at him. And if his hair was anything like the rest of him, he would probably be this way for years. So things didn't look good for Eugene.

"A dog?" my father said when he heard about it. "I can't believe it looks like a dog. Who says it looks like a dog?"

"The art teacher," Charlie said. "I heard her tell the principal. She said if it just wasn't on Eugene's head she would display it as an example of living sculpture."

"Why don't you tell that to Eugene?" Mother said. "It might make him feel better to know that he's a living sculpture."

I didn't think so. For one thing, nobody knew what a living sculpture was. I helped Eugene look it up in the encyclopedia, but we looked under *living* instead of *sculpture* and never got past *living sacrifice*, which was all about torture, and *that* sure didn't make Eugene feel better.

"Come on, Eugene," I said. "Don't be crazy. No one's going to make you be a sacrifice."

"Hah!" he said. "How about Gladys Herdman?"

He was really worried, and between being worried and short and having his hair all chopped up, Eugene began to twitch and wiggle and bite his fingernails and bang himself on the head.

"I can't help it," he said. "It makes me feel better."

Actually, there wasn't a kid in the Woodrow Wilson School who didn't wiggle or twitch or tie knots in his hair or *something*. Boomer Malone once ate a whole pencil without even knowing it till he got to the eraser and broke off a tooth. Some kids banged their heads, too, when they didn't have anything else to do, and of course the Herdmans banged *other* kids on the head, but nobody did it as hard as Eugene.

This was fascinating to Gladys Herdman. She quit hitting him and hollering at him and just followed him around everywhere— waiting for him to knock himself out, we all thought.

"Why do you do that all the time?" she asked him, but Eugene was scared to tell her the truth. He figured if he said, "It makes me feel better," she would pound him black and blue and claim it was a good deed.

My mother thought Eugene ought to enter the talent show. "It would take his mind off his troubles," she said, "and there must be *something* he could do."

I couldn't imagine what, except maybe stand up on the stage and be short, and I never heard of a show where part of the entertainment was somebody being short. So I was pretty surprised, along with everybody else, to learn that Eugene had a hidden talent that he would perform at the talent show.

"And then on TV, probably," Gladys Herdman said. Gladys was the one who discovered this talent but she wouldn't tell anybody what it was and she wouldn't let Eugene tell anybody either, not even his mother—so Mrs. Preston didn't know whether to get him a costume or a guitar or elevator shoes or what.

My mother didn't know what to put on the stage for him to use. "Maybe he needs a microphone," she said. "Maybe he needs some special music. I'd really like to know, because I want Eugene to be a success." It would be wonderful, she told us, if Eugene could win first prize in the talent show.

What she really meant was, it would be

wonderful if *anybody* besides Alice Wendleken would win first prize for a change, but I knew that wouldn't happen unless Alice broke both her arms and couldn't play the piano.

I guess Charlie thought it was worth a try, though, because he asked Eugene what he needed for his talent act.

"He needs walnuts," Charlie reported, "but he says he'll bring his own. He doesn't want to. He's scared to be in the talent show, but he's more scared of Gladys."

"What's he going to do with walnuts?" Mother asked.

"I don't know. Unless . . . maybe he's going to juggle them." Charlie brightened up. "That would be good! Even if he drops some, that would be good!"

It seemed to me that if Eugene could juggle *anything* we would all know about it, but maybe not. My friend Betty Lou Sampson is double-jointed and can fold herself into a pretzel, but she won't do it in front of people, because of being shy. It could be the same way with Eugene, I thought.

I also thought he might back out, but on the night of the talent show there he was, so for once we had something different to look forward to.

There isn't usually anything different or surprising about the talent show. One year a girl named Bernice Potts signed up to do an animal act and the animal turned out to be a goldfish, which was different. But then the act turned out to be Bernice talking to the fish and the fish talking back and Bernice telling the audience what the fish said. Charlie loved this, but he was in the first grade then and believed anything anybody told him.

Mrs. Wendleken said this act didn't belong in the talent show because it didn't have anything to do with human talent. "Even if the fish *could* talk," she said, "that would just mean the fish was talented, not Bernice."

Mrs. Wendleken didn't think Eugene should be juggling walnuts either, according to Alice. "If he can do it," Alice sniffed, "which he probably can't."

Eugene didn't even try. He came out on the stage carrying a big bowl of walnuts while Mother was introducing him. "Our next talented performer," she said, "is from the second grade. It's Eugene Preston, and Eugene is going to—"

Mother never got a chance to finish, because Eugene began smashing walnuts on his forehead one after another, just as fast as he could, and walnut shells flew everywhere.

People sitting in the back of the auditorium couldn't figure out what he was doing, and people sitting in the front of the auditorium knew what he was doing but couldn't believe he was doing it. The principal, who was sitting in the back row, thought kids were throwing things at Eugene, so he started up the aisle and ran smack into Mrs. Preston, who was yelling for someone to stop Eugene before he killed himself with walnuts.

Nobody heard her. There was too much noise. Kids were jumping up and down and clapping and hollering, "Go, Eugene! Go, Eugene!" and then, "Go, Hammerhead! Go, Hammerhead!" Boomer Malone began counting walnuts: ". . . twenty-two, twenty-three, twenty-four . . ." And pretty soon everybody was chanting, ". . . thirty-six, thirty-seven, thirty-eight . . ." Boomer said Mrs. Preston fainted when Eugene got to forty-five walnuts, but she didn't really faint. She just collapsed onto a seat, moaning something about "scrambled brains."

Eugene used all his walnuts and then he set his bowl down on the stage and walked off. He looked taller to me, but that's probably because I was looking up at him for a change.

Eugene didn't win first prize, but neither did Alice. Her piano solo was called "Flying Fingers," and it would have been pretty flashy except that there were so many walnut shells stuck in the piano keys that she kept having to stop and start over. Eugene was the popular favorite, but I guess the judges didn't want to reward a scramble-your-brains act, in case that *did* eventually happen to him, so they gave the first prize to the kindergarten rhythm band, which was probably the best thing to do. It made all the kindergarten mothers happy and it didn't make anyone else very mad.

Of course, kids were all over Eugene, telling him that he should have won, that he was the best, and wanting to feel his head.

"Did you always crack nuts that way?" someone asked, and Eugene said no, that it was Gladys Herdman's idea.

"Why?" Charlie said. "What was in it for Gladys?"

If you didn't know any better you might think that Gladys felt guilty because of Eugene's dog haircut, but no one at the Woodrow Wilson School would think that. So when we went to get the delicious refreshments, no one was very surprised to find they were all gone.

Mrs. McCluskey was in charge of the food, and when Mother asked her what happened she said, "I'd just put the last plate of cupcakes on the table when Gladys Herdman ran in here yelling that Eugene Preston had gone crazy in the auditorium and was trying to kill himself. Now normally I wouldn't pay any attention to *anything* a Herdman told me, but I could hear a lot of noise and stamping around and people yelling, 'Eugene! Eugene!' so naturally I went to see." She shrugged. "I still don't know what happened to Eugene, but I know what happened to the refreshments."

Everybody knew what happened to the refreshments but as usual you couldn't prove anything because the evidence was gone and Gladys was gone.

Mrs. Wendleken didn't agree. She said the evidence was Eugene. "It's obvious that Gladys Herdman got that poor little boy to knock himself silly and cause a big commotion, and then she went to the cafeteria and walked off with every last cookie!"

Maybe so, but Eugene *didn't* knock himself silly and you couldn't feel very sorry for him because he was a big celebrity with his name in the newspaper—"UNUSUAL PERFORMANCE BY PLUCKY EUGENE PRESTON EARNS STANDING OVATION AT WOODROW WILSON TALENT SHOW." The article also mentioned the kindergarten rhythm band, but not by name ("Too many of them," the reporter said) and not by musical number ("Could have been almost anything").

Besides, Eugene wasn't even Eugene anymore except to his mother and the teachers. And sometimes even the teachers forgot and called him Hammerhead, just like everyone else.

5

Every now and then I would remember about the assignment for the year—Compliments for Classmates—and turn to that page in my notebook. So far I had thought up compliments for six people, including Alice. For Alice, I put down "Important."

"I'm not sure I'd call that a compliment," my mother said.

"Alice would," I told her. Actually, Alice would probably consider it just a natural fact, like "The earth is round," "The sky is blue,"

"Alice Wendleken is important."

Alice began being important right away in the first grade because she was the only first-grade kid who had ever been inside the teachers' room. So whenever something had to be delivered there, Alice got to deliver it.

"I have a note to go to the teachers' room," our teacher would say, "way up on the third floor, so Alice, I'll ask you to be my messenger since you know exactly where it is."

Then Alice would stand up and straighten her dress and pat her hair and carry the note in both hands out in front of her as if it was news from God. Most of all, she would never tell what was in the room.

Whenever the teachers didn't have anything else to do, they went and hid in the teachers' room, but nobody else ever got in there. You couldn't *see* in, either, because the door was wood and frosted glass almost to the top.

Boomer Malone once got Charlie to climb on his shoulders and look in, but all Charlie could see was a sign that said "Thank God It's Friday," and another sign that said "Thank God It's June."

This got spread around school, and kids went home and told about the swear words in the teachers' room, so after that they put up a curtain and nobody could see anything.

"There isn't anything to see," my mother said.

"Just some chairs and tables and a sofa and a big coffeepot and a little refrigerator."

"No TV?" Charlie said.

"No TV."

"What do they do in there?"

Mother sighed. "I suppose they relax," she said, "and talk to each other, and have lunch."

"That's not what Imogene Herdman says," Charlie muttered.

"Well," Mother said, "if you believe what

Imogene Herdman says, you"ll believe any-thing."

"They go in there to smoke cigarettes and drink Cokes" was what Imogene had said. "And if somebody has a cake, they put it in a Sears, Roebuck sack and pretend it's some-thing they bought, and then they go in there and eat it where nobody can see them. And they don't let anybody in who doesn't know the password."

Charlie brightened right up. "What's the password?"

"They pick a new one every day," Imogene said, "and then they put it in the morning announcements, like in what's for lunch. Once it was *macaroni and cheese*."

I figured Imogene was making this up as she went along, so you had to be impressed with her imagination. I even got out my note-book and started to write that down: Imogene Herdman—"Has imagination." But then I realized it wasn't imagination, it was just a big lie. I also realized that finding a compliment for Imogene Herdman was probably the hardest thing I'd have to do all year and I'd better start thinking about it.

Of course, Charlie kept waiting for "macaroni and cheese" to show up in the morning announcements. He was going to walk past the teachers' room and say "macaroni and cheese" and see what happened. But the next time it was on the lunch menu, Charlie was stuck in the nurse's room with a nosebleed and didn't get to try it.

Imogene told him it didn't make any difference because the password that day was *softball*.

"Did you try it?" Charlie asked. "Did you get in?"

"I don't want in." Imogene gave him this dark, squinty-eyed look. "If a kid gets in that room, they never let him out. Remember Pauline Ellison?"

Charlie shook his head.

"Neither does anyone else. She got in the

teachers' room. Remember Kenneth Weaver? Did you see Kenneth Weaver lately?"

"No, because he's got the mumps."

"That's what you think. Kenneth doesn't have the mumps. Kenneth got caught in the teachers' room."

I guess this was too much, even for Charlie. "I don't believe you," he said.

Imogene grinned her girl-Godzilla grin. "Neither did Kenneth," she said. "I told him he better not go near the teachers' room but"—she shrugged—"he did it anyway."

For once nobody believed Imogene. Nobody *told* her so, but Alice Wendleken said that from now on Imogene couldn't shove people around anymore because she was a proven liar, and no matter what she said everybody would laugh at her and maybe knock her down. Nobody believed *that* either, but it sounded great.

"Just wait till Kenneth comes back!" everybody said. But Kenneth didn't come back.

Charlie hunted me up at recess with this news. "He's never coming back," he said. "The teacher gathered up his books and moved Bernadette Slocum into his seat and said, 'Well, we'll certainly miss Kenneth, won't we?' It's just like Imogene said!"

"Oh, come on, Charlie," I said. "You know they haven't got him shut up in the teachers' room."

Still . . . you had to wonder. First Imogene said Kenneth was gone, and then he *was* gone. What if Imogene was right?

I wasn't the only one who thought about this, and I wasn't the only one who found reasons to stay away from the teachers' room, and even to stay away from the whole third floor. Kids suddenly couldn't climb stairs for one reason or another or kids got dizzy if they went above the second floor. Alice had what she called a twisted toe and limped around holding on to chairs and tables, all on one floor, naturally.

But Louella McCluskey told the real truth, for everyone. "I don't *think* Imogene Herdman is right," she said, "and I don't *think* kids disappear into the teachers' room, but maybe she is and maybe they do, and I'm not going to take any chances."

Then two teachers and a district supervisor and Mrs. Wendleken all got locked in the teachers' room by accident. They were in there for an hour and a half, banging on the door and yelling and even throwing things out the window. They took down the curtain and climbed up on chairs and waved their arms around at the top of the door, but nobody saw them and nobody heard them because nobody ever went near the teachers' room.

They were all pretty mad, especially the district supervisor, and Mrs. Wendleken was hysterical by the time somebody let them out. By that time, too they were all worn out and hoarse from yelling and dizzy from waving their arms around in the air.

Who finally let them out was Imogene.

She said that she stood around trying to decide what to do, and that made Mrs. Wendleken hysterical all over again. "What to do!" she said.

"Open the door and let us out is what to do!"

"But it's the teachers' room," Imogene said, looking shocked, as if she had this rule burned into her brain. "We're not allowed in the teachers' room."

"You're allowed to let people *out* of the teachers' room!" Mrs. Wendleken hollered.

Then the district supervisor got mad at Mrs. Wendleken. "This child has saved the day," she said. "We ought to thank her. And let me tell you, there are plenty of schools in this district where the students spend every waking minute trying to break into the teachers' room, or sneak into the teachers' room.

You wouldn't believe the wild tales I've heard. Now here's a student who seems to understand that teachers need a little privacy. I hope you have more boys and girls like . . . is it Imogene?"

"We have five more exactly like her," one of the teachers said.

The district supervisor said that was wonderful and nobody argued with her—too tired, I guess, from jumping up and down yelling for help.

This whole thing got in the newspaper. "SCHOOL PERSONNEL LOCKED IN THIRD FLOOR ROOM," it said. "RELEASED BY ALERT STUDENT." It didn't name the alert student but it named everybody else who was there.

"Except Kenneth Weaver," Charlie said.. "It doesn't say anything about Kenneth Weaver."

"That proves it, Charlie," I said. "He never was in there."

"Why in the world would Kenneth Weaver be in the teachers' room?" Mother said. "That whole family moved to Toledo."

"Did they take Kenneth?" Charlie asked.

"Certainly they took Kenneth! Who would move away and leave their children?"

"Mr. Herdman," I said, but Mother said that was different.

Alice Wendleken cut out the newspaper article and gave it to Imogene. "I thought you'd want to keep it," she said, "since it's about you. Of course nobody knows it's about you because they didn't print your name. I wonder why they didn't print your name."

"They didn't print Kenneth's name either," Imogene said. "So what?"

"So Kenneth wasn't there!" Alice said.

Imogene stuck her nose right up against Alice's nose, which naturally made Alice nervous and also cross-eyed. "Why do you think I opened the door to that room?" she said.

"You think I opened the door to let all those teachers out? Who cares if they never get out? I let Kenneth out."

"My mother was in there," Alice said, "and she didn't see Kenneth."

"Did you ask her?"

"No, because I know Kenneth Weaver is in Toledo."

"He is now," Imogene said.

This was typical Herdman—too shifty to figure out, and Alice didn't even try.

Aside from congratulating Imogene, the district supervisor said that the worst part of being shut up in there for an hour and a half was the furniture. "Lumpy old sofa," she said, "broken-down chairs, terrible lighting. It doesn't surprise me that the door was broken. Everything in that room is broken."

So the teachers got a new sofa and chairs, and the furniture store donated a new rug, and they painted the walls and fixed the door and bought new curtains and a big green plant.

They left the door open too for a couple of days so everybody could see the new stuff, which just went to prove, Alice said, "that there's nobody hidden there and never was."

Imogene shrugged. "Suit yourself."

Charlie was feeling brave too. "Where would they be?" he said. "There's no place for them."

"Sure there is." Imogene pointed. "How about that? The plant that ate Chicago."

"The plant?" Mother said that evening. "Well, I would have chosen some normal kind of plant like a fern, but I guess they wanted something scientific for the teachers' room. That plant is a Venus's flytrap. It eats flies . . . swallows them right up."

Charlie looked at me, his eyes wide, and I knew what he was thinking—that maybe you could say the password by accident, disappear into the teachers' room, and never be seen again because of death by plant.

"It eats *flies*, Charlie," I said. "Nothing but flies."

"Well, after all, it's just a plant," Mother said. "It doesn't know flies from hamburger. I guess it eats anything it can get hold of."

Once Charlie spread that word around, you would normally have had kids lining up to feed stuff to the plant—pizza, potato chips, M&M cookies—and they would probably have had to keep the door locked and put up a big sign that said "Private, Keep Out, Teachers Only." But none of this happened because nobody would go near the teachers' room, not even to watch a plant eat lunch.

When the district supervisor came back to see the new furniture, she mentioned this and said that the teachers could thank "that thoughtful girl. What was her name? Imogene" for all this peace and privacy.

I guess she was right, in a way, but I didn't see any teachers rushing to thank Imogene. And never mind how much I needed to find a compliment for her, I certainly couldn't write down "Imogene Herdman is thoughtful," no matter what the district supervisor said.

6

Once a year we had to take an IQ test and a psychology test and an aptitude test, which showed what you might grow up to be if the Herdmans let you get out of the Woodrow Wilson School alive. But the only test the Herdmans ever bothered to take was the eye test.

This surprised everybody, because it meant that at least they knew the letters of the alphabet. You had to cover up one eye with a little piece of paper and read the letters on a chart, and then cover up the other eye and read them again. If you couldn't do it, it meant that you had to have glasses.

Sometimes it just meant that you were scared, like Lester Yeagle.

"If you don't do it right," Gladys Herdman told Lester, "it means your eyes are in backward, and they have to take them out and put them in the other way."

This made Lester so nervous that he couldn't tell *L* from *M* or *X* from *K* and when the doctor said, "Well, let's just switch eyes," he went all to pieces and had to go lie down in the nurse's room till his mother could come and get him.

Besides having three other kids and a baby, Mrs. Yeagle was a schoolbus driver, so she couldn't waste much time just letting Lester be hysterical. But Lester was too hysterical to tell her what happened—all he said was "Herdman."

"Which one?" Mrs. Yeagle said. "Which one did it?" and Lester said Gladys did it.

"Did what?" the nurse wanted to know. "Gladys wasn't even there."

"I don't know what," Mrs. Yeagle said, "and I can't wait around to find out because I had to leave the baby with the Avon lady and it's almost time to drive the bus. Come on, Lester, honey . . . maybe you can find out," she told the nurse.

Of course Gladys said she didn't do anything, and the eye doctor said *he* certainly didn't do anything. "But I got a look at that kid's braces," he said, "and I'll bet that's his problem."

I didn't think so. Having braces was no problem—*not* having braces was a problem. Gloria Coburn's little sister got braces and Gloria didn't, and Gloria cried and carried on for weeks. "I'll grow up ugly with an overbite," she said, and she didn't even know for sure what one was. She just wanted braces like everyone else.

That night the nurse called Mrs. Yeagle to say that apparently Gladys didn't do anything to Lester. "We think the trouble may be his braces," she suggested.

"What braces?" Mrs. Yeagle said. "Lester doesn't have braces." But then she went and looked in his mouth and she nearly died.

"What have you got in there?" she yelled. "What is all that? It looks like paper clips!"

Sure enough, Lester had paper clips bent around his teeth and he got hysterical all over again because his mother pried them off.

The nurse said she never heard of paper clips, "but you know they all want to have braces or bands or something. And they don't know how much braces cost."

"Well, these cost thirty-five cents," Mrs. Yeagle said. "According to Lester, Gladys Herdman put them on him and that's what she charged him. And let me tell you, that kid better never try to get on my bus! Or any other Herdmans either!"

Getting thrown off the bus was almost the worst thing that could happen to you. You had to go to school anyway, no matter what, so if you got thrown off the bus it meant that your father had to hang around and take you, or your mother had to stop whatever she was doing and take you, so you got yelled at right and left. You even got yelled at when it happened to someone else—"Don't *you* get thrown off the bus!" your mother would say.

Mrs. Herdman probably never said this, but she didn't have to worry about it anyway. The Herdmans never got thrown off a bus because nobody ever let them on one. Sometimes, though, they would hang around what would have been their bus stop if they had one, smoking cigars and starting fights and telling little kids that the bus was full of bugs.

"Big bugs," Gladys told Maxine Cooper's little brother, Donald. "Didn't you ever hear them? They chomp through anything to get food. You better give me your lunch, Donald. I'll take it to school for you."

Of course that was the end of Donald's lunch, but at least, Maxine said, it was just a day-old bologna sandwich and some carrot sticks so they probably wouldn't do that again.

"They're just jealous," Alice told her, "because they have to walk while everybody else gets to ride and be warm and comfortable."

"Come on, Alice," I said. "If you think the schoolbus is warm and comfortable, you must be out of your mind."

But Imogene Herdman was standing right behind us, so Alice ignored me and said again how wonderful it was to ride the schoolbus, and how she would hate to be the Herdmans who *couldn't* ride the schoolbus because they were so awful.

After that they began to show up every morning at Maxine's bus stop, looking sneaky and dangerous, like some outlaw gang about to hold up the stagecoach.

"But they don't do anything," Maxine said, looking worried. "They just stand around. It's scary."

It scared Donald, all right, and after three or four days he wouldn't even come out the door, so Maxine stood on her front porch and yelled, "My mother says for you to go home!"

"We can't go home!" Imogene yelled back. "We have to go to school."

Then they all nodded at each other, Maxine said, just as if they were this big normal family of ordinary kids who got up and brushed their teeth and combed their hair and marched out ready to learn something.

Maxine felt pretty safe on her own porch, so she said, "Then why don't you just get on the bus and go!"

"Get on *your* bus?" Imogene said. "Get on Bus Six?" And Gladys hollered that she wouldn't get on Bus 6 if it was the last bus in the world, and Leroy said, "Me neither."

"And then when the bus came," Maxine told us, "they all ran behind the McCarthys' front hedge and just stood there, staring at us."

"What did Mrs. Yeagle do?" I asked.

"She yelled at them, 'Don't you kids even think about getting on my bus!' and Ollie said, 'I'll never get on Bus Six!' He said it twice. Listen . . ." Maxine leaned forward and lowered her voice. "I think the Herdmans are scared of the bus."

This was the craziest thing I'd ever heard. "It's just a bus," I said.

"I *know* that," Maxine said, "but it's my bus and I have to ride on it, and I don't want to ride on a doomed bus!"

This sounded crazy too, but nobody

laughed, because if the Herdmans *were* scared of Bus 6, it was the *only* thing in the world they were scared of, so you had to figure they must know something no one else knew.

Whatever it was, they weren't telling, but every day there they were at the bus stop, whispering and shaking their heads.

Charlie thought they were stealing pieces of the bus, one little piece at a time, and someday the whole bus would just fall apart and scatter kids all over the street.

Eugene Preston brought in a copy of *Amazing Comics*, about a robot bus that suddenly began to go backward and sideways and turn itself over and lock all its doors, so the people were trapped inside, yelling and screaming. In the comic book the Mighty Marvo showed up and rescued everybody, but Eugene said he wouldn't want to count on the Mighty Marvo if he was up against the Herdmans.

"I just know something's going to happen," Maxine said. "I keep hearing this strange noise on the bus."

I don't know how she would hear anything except kids hollering, but Eloise Albright said she heard a strange noise too. Some kids said they smelled something on the bus, but who doesn't?—egg sandwiches, poison ivy medicine, Alice Wendleken's Little Princess perfume.

Lester finally asked his mother if there was anything wrong with their bus, but she just said, "Yes, it's full of kids."

Then Bus 6 was assigned to take the third grade to a dairy farm to study cows, and Ollie Herdman refused to go. "Not me," Ollie said. "Not on *that* bus!"

Of course this was good news for the cows, and the teacher was pretty happy, but the rest of the third grade was scared to death. Boomer Malone's little sister Gwenda said the suspense was awful—waiting for the bus to blow up or turn over—and between that and having to milk a cow, the whole third grade was wiped out for the rest of the day.

By this time Maxine was a nervous wreck, along with Donald and Lester and everybody else on Bus 6. More and more kids were feeling sick to their stomachs and then feeling fine as soon as the bus left, and they all said the same thing—that they were scared to ride the bus because the Herdmans wouldn't get on it.

"What kind of reason is that?" my mother wanted to know. "Of course they won't get on the bus. Thelma Yeagle won't *let* them on the bus. Nobody *wants* them on the bus!"

"Something bad is going to happen," Charlie told her, "and the Herdmans know what it is. That's why they won't get on. They know Bus Six is doomed."

"Doomed!" Mother stared at him. "You

watch too much television. Is that what everybody thinks?"

We said yes.

"Then why doesn't somebody just put the Herdmans on the bus and make them ride it?" Mother said.

Since it wasn't my bus, I thought that was a good idea and so did Charlie and so did Mr. Crabtree, I guess, because that's what he did.

"We have to ride your bus, Lester," Gladys said. She grinned this big grin so Lester could see her teeth all shiny with paper clips. "The principal said."

"I thought you were scared to ride this bus," Maxine told Imogene. "You said it was doomed."

"I didn't say that," Imogene told her. "*You* said that." She climbed on the bus and walked up and down the aisle, picking out a seat next to some victim. "It looks all right to me."

Mrs. Yeagle was pretty mad at first, but she told my mother it wasn't all bad to have the Herdmans on the bus. "They told everybody to shut up," she said, "and everybody did."

Not for long, though. Claude and Leroy stole a bunch of baby turtles from the pet store and took them on the bus and put them down some kids' shirts. Leroy said later that he was amazed at what happened. He thought the turtles were dead and he was going to take them back to the pet store and complain.

The turtles weren't dead. They probably saw who had them and decided to stay in their shells till they were big enough to bite back. But it was nice and warm inside the shirts, so they began to stick their heads out and crawl around.

Of course nobody knew they had turtles down their backs. Nobody knew *what* they had down their backs, but Donald Cooper thought it was the big bugs, hungry and tired of peanut butter sandwiches. "I've got the big bugs on me!" he yelled, and right away all the other kids began to yell and scream and jump up and down and thrash around so Mrs. Yeagle had to stop the bus and get everybody settled down.

It was another week before all the turtles came out from under the seats and behind the seat backs, so it was a good thing that they were little to begin with and didn't grow very fast.

Once the Herdmans had collected all the turtles, they got off the bus and never came back. "Don't want to ride this dumb bus," Ralph muttered, and I guess that was the real truth. They just wanted to get *on* the bus, take over the territory, wham a few kids, pick out the best lunch (Gwenda Malone's, usually, because Gwenda always had two desserts and no healthy food), and then get *off* the bus and stay off, which they did.

For once, though, they weren't the only ones who got what they wanted. Lester's baby teeth fell out like popcorn—"All those paper clips," Mrs. Yeagle said—and his second teeth came in all crooked and sideways, so he had more braces and bigger braces and fancier braces than anybody else in the Woodrow Wilson School, and maybe the whole world.

7

When Louella McCluskey's mother went to work part-time at the telephone company, she let Louella baby-sit her little brother, Howard, again during spring vacation.

"Just don't you let the Herdmans get him this time," she said. "He's got hair now so they can't draw all over his head but I don't know what else they might do."

Howard had hair all right, but it was no big improvement because it started way above his ears and grew straight up, like grass.

"If it was up to me," Louella said, "I'd shave his head and let him start all over."

"Just mention that to Leroy," I said.

Louella turned pale. "My mother would kill me, and I'd never get to watch television or go to the movies for the rest of my life."

Louella kept Howard out of sight for the whole time, but when school started again, the regular baby-sitter quit, so Mrs. McCluskey got special permission for Louella to bring Howard to school—"Just for a few days," she said. "Just till I find someone else."

"Now what'll I do?" Louella said. "I can't learn compound fractions and watch out for Howard all the time, and he'll be right there in the same room with Imogene Herdman!"

She was really worried and you couldn't blame her, so I wasn't too surprised when she showed up with Howard on a leash.

Miss Kemp was pretty surprised, though. "Is that necessary, Louella?" she asked. "After all, your little brother is our guest here in the sixth grade. Is that how we want to treat a guest, class?"

Some kids said no, but a lot of kids said yes because they figured Howard was going to be a pain in the neck. So then Miss Kemp spent ten minutes talking about manners and hospitality, but I guess *she* figured Howard might be a pain in the neck too because she didn't make Louella untie him.

She did make her get a longer leash, though, because Howard got knocked on his bottom every time he tried to go somewhere.

"He better learn not to do that," Imogene Herdman said. "Claude had to learn not to do that."

Miss Kemp looked at her. "Not to do what?"

"Not to go past the end of his leash."

"Why was Claude on a leash?"

"Because we didn't have a dog," Imogene said.

Miss Kemp frowned and sort of shook her head—the way you do when you've got water in your ears and everything sounds strange and faraway—but she didn't ask to hear any more and you couldn't blame her.

Louella poked me. "If they wanted a dog," she said, "they could just go to the Animal Rescue. That's where we got our dog."

That might be okay for Louella, but I didn't think the Animal Rescue people would give the Herdmans a rescued goldfish, let alone a whole dog, and the Herdmans probably knew it.

Maybe they even went there and said, "We want a dog," and the Animal Rescue said, "Not on your life." So then, I guess, they just looked around and said, "Okay, Claude, you be the dog," and then Claude was the dog till he got tired of it or they got tired of it.

You had to wonder what he *did* when he was the dog—bite people, maybe, except they had Gladys to do that.

Boomer Malone thought he might bark and guard the house.

"From what?" I asked.

Boomer shrugged. "I don't know . . . robbers?"

"Boomer, who are the main robbers around here?"

"Oh, yeah." He nodded. "They are."

Kids who *didn't* have dogs thought he might come when somebody called him, or sit up and beg, or roll over, or fetch papers. Kids who *did* have dogs said their dogs barked to get in and barked to get out, and chased cars, and swiped food off the table, and tore up the neighbors' trash, and all those things sounded more like Claude. You could see, though, how he would get tired of it.

"He probably got tired of being on a leash," Alice said. "Not like *some* people I know." She meant Howard. Alice had already told Louella what she thought about Howard. "I tried to teach your little brother to read," she'd said, "so he would be ready for kindergarten like I was. But I don't think they'll even let him *in* kindergarten. He's pretty dumb."

"He's too little to be dumb," Louella grumbled. "If you want to teach him something, you could teach him to go to the bathroom."

Well, I knew that wouldn't happen because Alice won't even say the word *bathroom*. It's a good thing you can just raise your hand to be excused, because if Alice had to say where she was going she would never go, and I don't know what would happen to her.

Dumb or not, Howard was okay for such a little kid stuck in the sixth grade. He had lots of paper and crayons, and little boxes of cereal to eat, and different people brought him different things to play with and look at. Alice showed up with great big pieces of cardboard that said *A* and *B* and *C*, but Howard didn't like those much. He scribbled all over them, which, Alice said, just proved how dumb he was, that he didn't even recognize the alphabet. "He'll never get into kindergarten," she said again. To hear Alice, you would think getting into kindergarten was better than getting into heaven, and a whole lot harder.

"They'll never let him in with *that*!" she said the first time she saw Howard's blanket, and for once you had to think she might be right. Howard's blanket was gross. Louella said it used to be blue and it used to have bunnies on it, but now it just looked like my father's car-washing rag.

"He has to have it," Louella said. "If he didn't have his blanket, Miss Kemp would probably have to throw him out. If he doesn't have his blanket, he cries and yells and jumps up and down, and if he still doesn't have his blanket, he holds his breath and turns purple."

Right away Boomer Malone scooped up the blanket and sat on it, which would have caused a big argument except that everyone *wanted* to see Howard turn purple. It was recess and there was already a bunch of kids gathered around Howard at one end of the playground, and naturally more kids came to see what was going on, and by the time Howard quit hollering and began to hold his breath, half the Woodrow Wilson School was there, trying to see over and around people.

"What's he doing?" I heard someone say. "Is he purple yet?"

He wasn't, and I didn't think he would *live* to be purple, with his eyes popping and all his little head veins standing out.

"Louella," I said, "do something . . .

he's going to explode!"

"No, he won't, she said. "He never does. You can't explode from holding your breath. It's a scientific fact. He won't even pass out. You'll see."

I didn't want to see—what if Louella was wrong?—but it didn't matter anyway because all of a sudden Imogene Herdman charged up, shoving kids out of the way right and left, and began to pound on Louella.

"You said he would turn purple!" she said. "Look at him, he's not purple. I can't stand around here all day waiting for him to turn purple. Here, kid." She threw Howard his blanket and Howard let out this big loud shuddery sob. Then he went on sobbing and hiccuping and hugging his blanket while Imogene stalked off and the whole big crowd of kids grumbled at Louella as if it was her fault.

"I should just take his blanket away right

now," Louella said, "and let everybody look at him and that would be that. But as far as I know he never had to hold his breath two times so close together and I don't know what that would do to him."

I thought it would probably kill him, so I was glad she didn't do it, but I knew plenty of kids *would* do it if they got the chance.

My mother said it better not be me or Charlie if we knew what was good for us. "That poor child has been scribbled on and scrubbed with scouring powder. He's been bald and shiny-headed and now what hair he's got looks as if someone planted it. Isn't that enough for one little boy?"

Either Imogene agreed with my mother or else she had plans to exhibit Howard at some later date ("See the Amazing Purple Baby! 25 cents") and didn't want him used up. From then on she kept one eye on Howard and the other eye on his blanket, and when

Wesley Potter tried to snatch Howard's blanket, he never knew what hit him.

Imogene smacked Wesley flat and then stood him up and *held* him up by the ears and said, "You leave that blanket alone and you leave that kid alone or I'll wrap your whole head in chewing gum so tight they'll have to peel it off along with all your hair and your eyebrows and your lip skin and everything!"

That took care of Wesley and everybody else who heard it, but it made Louella nervous.

"Why is she being nice to Howard?" Louella said. "Why did she get his blanket back? That's twice she's gotten Howard's blanket back. Why?"

I didn't know why but I knew she wouldn't have to do it again because nobody wants to go through life wrapped in gum *or* skinned bald, and that would be your choice.

"Maybe she likes him," I said.

"Why would she like him?" Louella said.

"I don't even like him and he's my own brother."

"But that's normal," I said. "I'm not crazy about Charlie either. If Howard was somebody else's brother you'd like him. *I* like him. There's nothing not to like unless he *is* your brother and you have to bring him to school and watch out for him and keep him on a leash and all."

"Keep him on a leash . . ." Louella repeated. "Remember what Imogene said? They kept Claude on a leash because they didn't have a dog?"

"So?"

"Well, they still don't have a dog, and here's Howard already on a leash . . . O-o-h!" Louella squealed. "Imogene is going to make him be their dog and my mother will kill me!"

"Come on, Louella," I said. "You can't make a person be a dog. They could *pretend*

Howard is their dog, but. . .

"Just look at Howard," Louella said. "He'll pretend anything Imogene wants him to."

This was true. Howard was hugging his blanket and feeling his one favorite corner (which was even rattier than the whole rest of the blanket) and looking at Imogene the way you would look at the tooth fairy, handing out ten dollars a tooth.

"She'll feed him dog biscuits and teach him to bite!" Louella moaned.

"Maybe he'll bite Gladys," I said, "and there's nothing wrong with dog biscuits. Everybody eats dog biscuits at least once to see what they taste like."

I personally didn't care for them, but when Charlie was little he was crazy about this one brand called Puppy Pleasers. I once asked him how they tasted and he knew exactly.

"If you take a chocolate bar to the beach," he said, and put it in the sand and let it melt and then pick up the melted chocolate bar and the sand and stick it all in the freezer, and when it's frozen bust it up into little pieces, is how Puppy Pleasers taste."

At the time I thought Charlie would either die of grit or slowly turn to sand from the feet up and I didn't know what we would do with him—stand him up in the backyard, maybe, and plant flowers around him.

I didn't know what the Herdmans would do with their dog, Howard, either. Whenever Charlie and I asked for a dog, my mother always said, "What are you going to do with him?" and we never knew what to say. We thought the dog would do it all and we would just hang around and watch.

Mother said that's exactly what she *thought* we thought. "When you find a dog that's smart enough to take care of itself and let itself in and out of the house and answer the phone, let me know," she said.

Louella said we would have to watch Imogene, "Or else she'll try to run off with Howard and take him home and name him some dog name, like Rover or Spot."

Luckily, she never got the chance. Mrs. McCluskey got her wires crossed at the telephone company and shut down the whole system for half an hour. She never knew a thing like that could happen, she said, and it made her so nervous that she just quit her job, right on the spot. And after that Louella didn't have to bring Howard to school anymore.

This was a big relief to Louella and you could tell it made Miss Kemp happy too, but she gave a little speech anyway, about how we would miss Howard and how he would be a big part of our sixth-grade experience and how we would always remember him.

"Sounds like he died," Imogene muttered. She was mad, I thought, because of wasting all her good deeds—getting Howard's blanket back and making kids leave him alone—and then not getting anything for it, like a substitute dog, if that was what she wanted.

"There is one thing," Miss Kemp went on. "It seems Howard went off without his blanket. Has anyone seen Howard's blanket?"

No one had. Or else no one would *admit* they had, not with Imogene sitting there blowing this huge bubble of gum out and in and out and in, ready to park it on anyone who looked guilty. It's too bad you can't study bubble gum and get graded for it, because Imogene would get straight A's. Her bubbles were so big and so thin you could see her whole face through the bubble, like looking at somebody through their own skin.

"What if we can't find it?" I asked Louella.

"We better find it," she said, "or else

Howard will go crazy because all he does is sob and cry and hold his breath and hiccup."

He had also turned purple, she said, and he had almost passed out, so you had to figure that if somebody didn't turn up with Howard's blanket soon he would never make it to next week, let alone kindergarten.

We looked for the blanket off and on the rest of that day, although Alice said it would be better if we didn't find it. "It's old and horrible and full of germs," she said, and she told Louella, "You should be glad it's lost. Howard will thank you someday."

This is what your mother says when she makes you wear ugly shoes. She says, "This will give your toes room to grow and you'll thank me someday." Hearing Alice say things like this makes you want to squirt her with canned cheese. Even Miss Kemp does, I think, because she said, "Alice, I can assure you that by the time Howard gets to 'someday,' he won't even *remember* this blanket."

Somebody muttered, "Don't be too sure"—Imogene.

There was good news the next day—Howard had lived through the night without going crazy *or* purple—and even better news when Imogene showed up with his blanket. She said she found it at the bus stop underneath a bush.

Nobody believed this. The Herdmans stole everything that wasn't nailed down, just out of habit. Why not Howard's blanket? "But so what?" Louella said, as long as Imogene brought it back.

The next day the art teacher, Miss Harrison, stopped Louella in the hall and gave her a bunch of stubby crayons for Howard. "I just heard about your little brother's blanket," she said. "Louella, you aren't going to find it because I threw it away. The last time we had art I used it to wipe the pastels off the chalkboard and then I just threw it away. I'm really sorry, but I didn't know it was Howard's blanket. It looked like my car-washing rag."

Louella shook her head. "We found Howard's blanket."

Miss Harrison shook *her* head. "You're just saying that to make me feel better. No, as soon as I heard it was missing, I knew what I'd done and where it was—gone, in the trash."

"She's wrong," Louella said.

"Maybe you're wrong," I said.

Louella thought for a minute. "Well, Howard wouldn't be wrong and *he* thinks it's his blanket. You can't get it away from him."

We did get it away from him but we had to wait till he was asleep. Then we had to unfasten his fingers and quickly give him this old worn-out bathrobe of Louella's.

"See?" said Louella. "It's the same blanket."

It certainly looked like the same blanket—old, faded, sort of dirty gray, with one corner that was especially old and faded and dirty gray. There was something else too—a capital *H*, scribbled and wobbly and almost faded out.

"It even has his initial on it," I said. "*H*, for Howard."

"Huh-uh," Louella said. "There's no initial on Howard's blanket."

I started to show her the *H*, and then I saw the *other* initial. It was an *I*.

I.H. There was only one *I.H.* in the whole Woodrow Wilson School—Imogene Herdman. "Louella," I said, "Imogene didn't find this blanket underneath a bush or anywhere else. This was her *own* blanket."

Louella refused to believe this and you couldn't blame her. It was hard enough just to imagine that Imogene ever *was* a baby, let alone a baby with her own blanket to drag around and hang on to.

"Besides," Louella said, "if it was hers, she wouldn't give it away. The Herdmans never gave anything away in their whole life."

"But what about the initials?" I said.

"They aren't really initials," Louella said. "I think they're just what's left of the bunny pattern."

I guess Louella believed this, but I knew better. They were Imogene's initials, all right, and this was Imogene's blanket. Maybe somebody took it away from her when *she* was a baby, and maybe *she* yelled and held her breath and turned purple, so she would know exactly how Howard felt. She would be sympathetic.

I could hardly wait to write this down on the Compliments for Classmates page in my notebook, but it looked too weird: "Imogene Herdman—sympathetic."

Nobody would believe this and I would

have to explain it and Imogene would probably wrap *my* head in chewing gum if I told
everyone that she once had a blanket with a
favorite chewed corner and everything.

8

Two or three times a year all the Herdmans would be absent at the same time and it was like a vacation. You knew you wouldn't get killed at recess, you wouldn't have to hand over your lunch, and you wouldn't have to hide your money if you had any.

We even had easy lessons when they were absent. Boomer Malone said the teachers did that on purpose to give us all time to heal and get our strength back, but my mother said it was probably the teachers who had to get their strength back.

Nobody knew why they were absent. Nobody cared. They didn't have to bring a note from home either like everyone else, to say what was the matter.

"Why bother?" the school nurse told my mother. "They would write it themselves, no one could read it, and it would be a lie. Besides, if they ever did have something contagious, they wouldn't stay home. They'd come here and breathe on everybody."

You never knew *when* they would be absent either, but nobody thought this made any difference till they were all absent on a fire-drill day and our school won the Fire Department Speed and Safety Award.

"I can't believe this improvement," the fire chief said. "Last time it took you thirty-four minutes to vacate the building. What happened?"

"You know what happened," Mr. Crabtree said. "We lost half the kindergarten. Ollie Herdman led them out a basement door and took them all downtown."

"I mean, what happened this time?"

"Nothing happened this time," Mr. Crabtree said, "because Ollie isn't here. Neither is Ralph or Imogene or Leroy or Claude or Gladys."

"Where are they?"

"They're absent," Mr. Crabtree said.

The chief sighed. "I thought maybe they moved away. Oh, well . . ." He sighed again and said in that case he'd better get back to the firehouse and be ready for anything.

Everyone was pretty excited about the Speed and Safety Award, because we had never won anything before and probably never would again till the last Herdman was gone from Woodrow Wilson School.

So far, though, we could only be excited

about the honor of it because we wouldn't get the actual award till Fire Prevention Day. There was a Fire Prevention Day every year, but all we ever got were Smokey the Bear stickers, so this was a big step up. There would be a special assembly with the fire chief and the mayor there, and the newspaper would send someone to take pictures and interview kids about fire prevention.

Of course fire prevention was the last thing the Herdmans knew anything about—except to be against it, I guess—so you had to hope the reporter wouldn't pick one of them to interview. You had to hope they wouldn't show up for this big event wearing beer advertisement T-shirts. You had to hope they wouldn't *show up*.

"Maybe they won't," Charlie said. "Maybe they don't even know we won the award."

It's true that the Herdmans didn't know

much if you count things like who invented
the telephone, but they always knew what
was going on around them, which in this case
was plenty. There were signs and posters about
fires and firemen everywhere; all the black-
boards said "Woodrow Wilson Elementary
School, Speed and Safety Winner!" Kids were
making bookmarks and placemats, and writ-
ing poems and stories about our big accom-
plishment. We didn't even have hot dogs and
hamburgers at lunch—we had Fire Dogs and
Smokey Burgers.

How could the Herdmans miss all this?
They didn't.

Somebody in the second grade brought in
this great big stuffed bear and they stood it
up in the hall with a sign around its neck—
"Smokey says Congratulations to the
Woodrow Wilson School!"—and the very
next day there was the bear with its paws full
of matches and cigarette lighters, firecrackers

in its lap, and a half-smoked cigar sticking out of its mouth . . . Smokey, the Fire-Bug Bear.

"Oh, that is so disgusting!" Alice said. "What if someone reports it to the fire department? We might not even get the award. As usual, they're going to mess everything up and ruin the whole assembly, hitting people and tripping people and folding little kids up in the seats!"

I guess Mr. Crabtree came in the back door that day and didn't know what had happened to the bear, because the first announcement was all about the outstanding fire-prevention display by the second grade. "I want every student to stop by the second-grade room and see our very own Smokey the Bear," he said, "and let's be sure to thank those second graders for this . . ." Then there were some whispers and a *thwip* sound as somebody put a hand over the microphone, but you could still hear voices and a few words: ". . . matches . . .

horrible wet cigar . . . get rid of that bear . . ."

Then the secretary, Mrs. Parker, got on and shuffled some papers and cleared her throat and said that Mr. Crabtree had been called away suddenly and she would finish the announcements: Picture money was due by Friday; a Fred Flintstone lunch box had been left on Bus 4; there would be a meeting of the Fire Safety Team in the lunchroom after school.

Right away Alice wrote this down on a piece of paper, as if she had so many important engagements that she *had* to write them all down.

Imogene poked me. "What's the Fire Safety Team?"

"It's for the assembly," I said. "It's some kids who are going to demonstrate what to do in case of fire."

Imogene shrugged. "Throw water on it and get out of the way." Then she squinched up her eyes. "What kids? Who's on this team?"

I was going to say "I don't know" or "Who cares"—something so loose that Imogene wouldn't want to waste her time—but as usual Alice had to blow her own horn.

"I am," she said. "There's ten of us plus two alternates in case somebody gets sick at the last minute."

It's not unusual for people to get sick at the last minute if they're mixed up with Herdmans, so that got Imogene's attention, but it wasn't enough to hold her attention till Alice said, "We're going to have T-shirts that say 'Fire Safety Team, Woodrow Wilson School,' so we'll all look alike in the picture."

I didn't even bother to say "Shut up, Alice"—it was too late. You could tell that Imogene was already seeing herself in the Fire Safety T-shirt *and* in the picture, and there was only one thing that you didn't know for sure—who, besides the two alternates, was going to get sick at the last minute.

Naturally Imogene wasn't the only Herdman who showed up in the lunchroom after school. They were all there, slouching around ready for action, draped over the tables, scraping gum from underneath the benches, chewing it—and this was *old* gum, shiny with germs and hard enough to tear your teeth out.

There was at least one kid from every grade on the Fire Safety Team and they all had one eye on the Herdmans, so Mr. Crabtree couldn't just *ignore* them, which is probably what he wanted to do.

"School's over, Ralph," Mr. Crabtree said, "Imogene, Ollie. Unless you people have some reason to be here, it's time to go home. We're just having a meeting."

"We came to sign up," Ralph said.

"Sign up for what? This is the Fire Safety Team."

"Right," Leroy said. "That. We want to sign up for that."

"It was on the announcements," Gladys put in, "about the meeting after school."

Mr. Crabtree opened his mouth and then he shut it again because there wasn't anything he could do about this. He had made it a major rule that anybody at the Woodrow Wilson School could sign up for anything they wanted to, no exceptions, and he had made another rule that everybody had to sign up for something whether they wanted to or not. So you had kids who signed up for two or three things, and you had kids who signed up for everything, and you had kids who wouldn't sign up at all till their teacher or their mother or Mr. Crabtree made them be something. What you didn't have was Herdmans signing up for anything.

Till now.

My mother said it was a good idea for the

Herdmans to be on a Fire Safety Team. "Who needs to know more about fire safety than those kids?" she said. Some people said at least this way you could keep an eye on them during the assembly. My father said it was like inviting a lot of bank robbers to demonstrate how to rob the bank.

Three kids quit the Fire Safety Team right away before anything could happen to them, but their mothers said they ought to get the T-shirts anyway in view of the circumstances.

Mr. Crabtree knew what circumstances they were talking about—Herdmans—so he didn't even mention that. He just said he didn't have anything to do with the T-shirts. "That's up to the PTA," he said. "The PTA is providing T-shirts for the Fire Safety Team in honor of this special occasion."

The president of the PTA said they weren't providing T-shirts for kids who *quit* the Fire Safety Team. Mrs. Wendleken said they better not be providing T-shirts for the Herdmans, who had muscled their way *onto* the Fire Safety Team.

All anybody could talk about was T-shirts, but I agreed with Charlie, who said he wouldn't be on the Fire Safety Team if you paid him, not even for fifty T-shirts. "I watched them practice," he said, "and when Mr. Crabtree yells 'Drop and roll!' all the Herdmans drop *on* somebody, like in football."

They dropped on Albert Pelfrey and nearly squashed him flat, which wasn't all bad because as I said Albert is this really fat kid, but Albert quit the Fire Safety Team anyway. "I've got enough trouble just being fat," he said. "I don't want to be fat and dead both."

At the last minute two kids got sick (or said they did) and right away both the alternates quit, which didn't surprise anybody.

"You don't want to quit," Mr. Crabtree

told them. "This is a big opportunity." He meant it was a big opportunity to take part in Fire Prevention Day and get a T-shirt and have their picture taken. But it was also a big opportunity to get pounded two feet into the ground by the Herdmans.

"I can only be an alternate," Roberta Scott said. "I can't actually be in it or anything."

"Roberta, that's what an alternate is," Mr. Crabtree said. "It's your responsibility to be in it and everything. You too, Lonnie."

Lonnie Hutchison was the other alternate, and he said he had to quit because of his asthma.

"Nice try, Lonnie," Mr. Crabtree said, "but you don't have asthma. I know who all has asthma. I *know* who has pinkeye and poison ivy and athlete's foot, also coughs and colds and nervous stomachs."

Mr. Crabtree didn't mention any other diseases, and when Lonnie's mother called the school to say that Lonnie was sick with a rash, Mr. Crabtree didn't believe it.

"Too convenient," he said. "It's probably finger paint or Magic Marker, something like that. Two or three weeks ago I saw Leroy Herdman walking around with red spots all over *his* face, looking for trouble. I just told him, 'Leroy, go wash your face,' and the next time I saw him all the spots were gone."

But it wasn't finger paint on Lonnie.

It was chicken pox, and before you could say "Speed and Safety Award assembly" there wasn't anybody left to go to it.

Mr. Crabtree wanted to postpone Fire Prevention Day but the fire chief said he couldn't do that. "It's Fire Prevention Day all over town," he said, "all over the state. You can't just have your own Fire Prevention Day whenever you want to. Tell you what, though. If you'll get together a small group of whatever kids you've got left—your Fire

Safety Team would be good—and bring them down to the firehouse, we'll have the award presentation right here. We'll make it a big event."

It turned out to be a bigger event than anybody expected because the pizza-parlor ovens caught fire half an hour before the presentation. They put the fire out right away but Mr. Santoro made all his customers leave because of the smoke, and most of them just followed the fire engine back to the firehouse and stayed for the presentation. Some people thought the fire was *part* of the presentation, especially when Mr. Santoro showed up with all his leftover pizza and handed it out free.

Everybody said this was a great way to advertise fire prevention, and they congratulated the mayor and the fire chief for thinking it up, and the fire chief congratulated Mr. Santoro for donating the pizza.

The newspaper reporter got it all wrong

too. "MOCK FIRE STAGED TO HIGHLIGHT FIRE PREVENTION DAY," he wrote. "RESTAURANT OWNER CONTRIBUTES PIZZA FOR LARGE CROWD ATTENDING AWARD CEREMONY. SCHOOL STUDENTS HONORED FOR SAFETY TECHNIQUES."

The "honored students" were what was left of the Fire Safety Team—Ralph, Imogene, Leroy, Claude, Ollie, and Gladys—and there was a picture of them standing in front of the fire truck, looking like a police lineup. You could imagine an officer saying, "Now, which one did it?" and the victim saying, "I can't be sure. They all look alike."

They did look alike, except for being different sizes . . . plus, of course, they had on the famous matching T-shirts.

"If I didn't know better," Mother said, "I would think this was the Herdmans being honored instead of the school."

This turned out to be the general opinion, and so many people called the newspaper to

complain that they printed another story—
"WOODROW WILSON SCHOOL, DESPITE CHICKEN
POX EPIDEMIC, WINS SPEED AND SAFETY AWARD,"
which my father said was better than nothing,
but not much. "What does chicken pox have
to do with it?" he wanted to know, but my
mother said he was just tired of watching
Charlie and me scratch.

Mrs. Wendleken made Alice sit in a bathtub
full of baking-soda water so she wouldn't
scratch, and made her wear these white cotton
gloves so she wouldn't scratch, and when Alice
came back to school, besides having puckery
seersucker skin, she was still wearing the gloves.

"I don't think that's necessary, Alice,"
Miss Kemp said.

"I have to wear them while I'm thinking,"
Alice told her, "so I won't forget and scratch.
If you scratch chicken pox, they get infected
and leave scars."

"Not on Leroy," Imogene said. "Not on

Ollie. Not on . . ."

"Wait a minute," Miss Kemp said. "Leroy? Ollie? I wasn't aware that any of your family was absent during our epidemic."

"Oh, we weren't absent," Imogene said.

Miss Kemp frowned. "But you had chicken pox?" she asked.

"You mean, did I have chicken pox?" Imogene said.

This was like talking long distance to my grandmother without her hearing aid, and— just like my grandmother—Miss Kemp didn't try to pin it down.

"If you have chicken pox, you can't come back without a note from the doctor," she said, and Imogene said, "Oh. Okay," and got up and left.

So no one ever knew for sure whether they did actually have chicken pox, or how many of them had chicken pox, or exactly when they had chicken pox, and no one ever knew for sure whether they came to school and breathed on everybody and ruined our big award assembly, or whether they were all sick and stayed home on the fire-drill day so we won the award in the first place.

9

The last day of school is pretty loose and they probably wouldn't even bother to have one except that that's when you clean out your desk. If you didn't have to clean out your desk, Mr. Crabtree could just get on the PA system any old day in June and say, "All right, this is it, last day of school. Go on home. Have a great summer. See you in September."

But then everyone would go off and leave their smelly old socks and moldy mittens and melted Halloween candy and leftover sandwiches. Once a kindergarten gerbil got loose and climbed in Boomer Malone's desk and died there.

Nobody knew what to do with the gerbil because, like all the kindergarten animals, it had a name and a personality and we knew all about it from the notice on the bulletin board—"Our friendly gerbil is missing. His name is Bob. If you see Bob, please return him to the kindergarten room."

So this wasn't just any old dead gerbil— this was friendly Bob. It didn't seem right to drop him in the trash, so Boomer took him back to the kindergarten room. We all thought the kindergarten would stop whatever it was doing, hunt up a cigar box, write a poem for Bob, and have a funeral, but according to Boomer they couldn't care less.

"Not even the teacher," he reported. "She took one look and said, 'Oh, that's not Bob,' and dropped him in her trash basket."

If there was a moral to this, I guess it was: Don't show up with dead animals on the last day of school.

You couldn't show up with live ones either anymore. We used to have a pet parade every year on the last day of school, till the year Claude Herdman entered their cat.

The Herdmans' cat was missing one eye and part of an ear and most of its tail and all of whatever good nature it ever had, so you wouldn't expect it to win any prizes in a pet parade. If it was your cat, you would probably try to clean it up a little, but you probably wouldn't whitewash it and then spray it with super-super-hold hairspray, which is what the Herdmans did.

According to Claude, they thought it would win the Most Unusual Pet prize, but it was too mad from being whitewashed and hairsprayed to do anything but attack. So the pet parade turned into a stampede of dogs and cats and turtles and hamsters and guinea pigs. Some kids held on to their animals but most didn't, so there were cats up in the trees and on top of telephone poles, and dogs running off down the street, barking . . . and the Herdmans' cat in the middle of it all, tearing around the playground, hissing and spitting and shedding flakes of whitewash. It took all day to get the cats down and the dogs back, and there were two hamsters that never did turn up.

So that was the end of the pet parade, and it left a big empty spot in the day's activities, which the teachers had to fill up somehow. We had spelling bees and math marathons, or we stood up and said what we were going to do that summer, or what we would do if we were king of the world.

One year everybody brought their collections. There were baseball cards and Cracker

Jack prizes and bubble-gum wrappers . . . and belly-button lint.

The belly-button lint came from Imogene Herdman, but she said she wouldn't recommend it as a hobby. "I don't even collect it anymore," she said. "This is left over from when I *used* to collect it." I guess that was the last straw—old belly-button lint—because we never did that again.

This year there was no big surprise about what we would do on the last day. It was up on the blackboard—Compliments for Classmates—and we had each drawn a name from a hat and had to think of more compliments for that one person.

"We've been thinking about this all year," Miss Kemp said. She probably knew that some kids had but most kids hadn't—but now everybody would think about it in a hurry. "And on the last day of school," she went on, "we're going to find out what we've learned about ourselves and each other."

I had finally thought of a word for Albert. Once you get past thinking *fat* you can see that Albert's special quality is optimism, because Albert actually believes he will be thin someday, and says so. Another word could be *determination*, or even *courage*. There were lots of good words for Albert, so I really hoped I would draw his name.

I didn't. The name I drew was Imogene Herdman, and I had used up the one and only compliment I finally thought of for Imogene—*patriotic*.

"Patriotic?" my mother said. "What makes you think Imogene is especially patriotic?"

"When we do the Pledge of Allegiance," I said, "she always stands up."

"Everybody stands up," Charlie said. "If everybody sat down and *only* Imogene stood up, that would be patriotic."

"That would be brave," I said.

"Well, she would do that," Charlie said. "I mean, she would do whatever everybody else didn't do."

Would that make Imogene brave? I didn't really think so, but I had to have some more compliments, so I wrote it down—*patriotic, brave.*

Two days later I still had just *patriotic* and *brave* while other people had big long lists. I saw the bottom of Joanne Turner's list, sticking out of her notebook: "Cheerful, good sport, graceful, fair to everybody." I wondered who *that* was.

Maxine Cooper asked me how to spell *cooperative* and *enthusiastic*, so obviously she had a terrific list. Boomer must have drawn a boy's name, because all his compliments came right out of the Boy Scout Rules—*thrifty, clean, loyal.*

I kept my eye on Imogene as much as possible so if she did something good I wouldn't miss it, but it was so hard to tell, with her, what was good.

I thought it was good that she got Boyd Liggett's head out of the bike rack, but Mrs. Liggett didn't think so.

Mrs. Liggett said it was all the Herdmans' fault in the first place. "Ollie Herdman told Boyd to do it," she said, "and then that Gladys got him so scared and nervous that he couldn't get out, and then along came Imogene . . ."

I could understand how Boyd got his head *into* the bike rack—he's only in the first grade, plus he has a skinny head—but at first I didn't know why he couldn't get it *out*.

Then I saw why. It was his ears. Boyd's ears stuck right straight out from his head like handles, so his head and his ears were on one side of the bike rack and the rest of him was on the other side, and kids were hollering at him and telling him what to do. "Turn your head upside down!" somebody said, and somebody else told him to squint his eyes and squeeze his face together.

Boyd's sister Jolene tried to fold his ears and push them through but that didn't work, even one at a time. Then she wanted half of us to get in front of him and push and the other half to get in back and pull. "He got his head through there," she said. "There must be some way to get it back out."

I didn't think pushing and pulling was the way but Boyd looked ready to try anything.

Then Gladys Herdman really cheered him up. "Going to have to cut off your ears, Boyd," she said. "But maybe just one ear. Do you have a favorite one? That you like to hear out of?"

You could tell that he believed her. If you're in the first grade with your head stuck through the bike rack, this is the very thing you think will happen.

Several teachers heard Boyd yelling, "Don't cut my ears off!" and they went to tell Mr. Crabtree. Mr. Crabtree called the fire department, and while he was doing that the kindergarten teacher stuck her head out the window and called to Boyd, "Don't you worry, they're coming to cut you loose."

But she didn't say who, or how, and Gladys told him they would probably leave a little bit of ear in case he ever had to wear glasses, so Boyd was a total wreck when Imogene came along.

She wanted to know how he got in there—in case she ever wanted to shove somebody else in the bike rack, probably—but Boyd was too hysterical to tell her, and nobody else knew for sure, so I guess she decided to get him loose first and find out later.

Imogene Scotch-taped his ears down and buttered his whole head with soft margarine from the lunchroom, and then she just pushed on his head—first one side and then the other—and it slid through.

Of course Boyd was a mess, with butter all over his eyes and ears and up his nose, so Jolene had to take him home. She made him walk way away from her and she told him, "As soon as you see Mother, you yell, 'I'm all right. I'm all right.'" She looked at him again. "You better tell her who you are, too."

Even so, Mrs. Liggett took one look and screamed and would have fainted, Jolene said, except she heard Boyd telling her that he was all right.

"What do you think of that?" Mother asked my father that night. "She buttered his head!"

"I think it was resourceful," my father said. "Messy, but resourceful."

"That's like a compliment, isn't it?" I asked my father. "It's good to be resourceful?"

"Certainly," he said. So I wrote that down,

along with *patriotic* and *brave*.

I thought we would just hand in our compliment papers on the last day of school, but
Alice thought Miss Kemp would read three
or four out loud—"Some of the best ones,"
Alice said, meaning, of course, her own—and
Boomer thought she would read the different
compliments and we would have to guess the
person. So when Miss Kemp said, "Now
we're going to share these papers," it was no
big surprise.

But then she said, "I think we'll start with
Boomer. LaVerne Morgan drew your name,
Boomer. I want you to sit down in front of
LaVerne and listen to what she says about you."

LaVerne squealed and Boomer turned two
or three different shades of red and all over
the room kids began to check their papers in
case they would have to read out loud some
big lie or, worse, some really personal compliment.

LaVerne said that Boomer was smart and good at sports—but not stuck up about it—and friendly, and two or three other normal things. "And I liked when you took the gerbil back to the kindergarten that time," she said, "in case they wanted to bury it. That was nice."

It *was* nice, I thought, and not everybody would have done it, either. To begin with, not everybody would have *picked up* the gerbil by what was left of its tail, let alone carry it all the way down the hall and down the stairs to the kindergarten room.

"Good, Boomer," I said when he came back to his seat—glad to get there, I guess, because he was all sweaty with embarrassment from being told nice things about himself face to face and in front of everybody.

Next came Eloise Albright and then Louella and then Junior Jacobs and then Miss Kemp said, "Let's hear about you, Beth.

Joanne Turner drew your name."

I remembered Joanne Turner's paper—
"Cheerful, good sport, graceful, fair to everybody." I had wondered who that was.

It was me.

"I know we weren't supposed to say things
about how you look," Joanne said, "but I
put down graceful anyway because I always
notice how you stand up very straight and
walk like some kind of dancer. I don't know
if you can keep it up, but if you can I think
people will always admire the way you stand
and walk."

It was really hard, walking back to my seat
now that I was famous for it—but I knew if I
did it now, with everybody watching, I *could*
probably keep it up for the rest of my life and,
if Joanne was right, be admired forever. This
made me feel strange and loose and light, like
when you press your hands hard against the
sides of a door, and when you walk away your

hands float up in the air all by themselves.

I was still feeling that way three people later when Miss Kemp said it was Imogene's turn.

"To do what?" Imogene said.

"To hear what Beth has to say about you. She drew your name."

Imogene gave me this dark, suspicious look. "No, I don't want to."

"You're going to hear *good* things, you know, Imogene," Miss Kemp said, but you could tell Miss Kemp wasn't too sure about that, and Imogene probably never *heard* any good things about herself, so she wasn't too sure, either.

"That's okay," I said. "I mean, if Imogene doesn't want to, I don't care."

This didn't work. I guess Miss Kemp was curious like everybody else. "Imogene Herdman!" Louella had just whispered. "That's whose name you drew? How could you think of compliments for Imogene Herdman?"

"Well, you had to think of *one*," I said. "We had to think of one compliment for everybody."

Louella rolled her eyes. "I said she was healthy. I didn't know anything else to say."

Louella wasn't the only one who wanted to hear my Imogene words. The whole room got very quiet and I was glad, now, that at the last minute I had looked up *resourceful* in the dictionary.

"I put down that you're patriotic," I told Imogene, "and brave and resourceful . . . and cunning and shrewd and creative, and enterprising and sharp and inventive . . ."

"Wait!" she yelled. "Wait a minute! Start over!"

"Oh, honestly!" Alice put in. "You just copied that out of the dictionary! They're all the same thing!"

"And," I went on, ignoring Alice, "I think it was good that you got Boyd's head out of the bike rack."

"Oh, honestly!" Alice said again, but Miss Kemp shut her up.

Of course she didn't say, "Shut up, Alice"—she just said that no one could really comment on what anybody else said because it was very personal and individual. "That's how Beth sees Imogene," she said.

Actually, it wasn't. Alice was right about the words. I did copy them out of the dictionary so I wouldn't be the only person with three dumb compliments, and I didn't exactly connect them with Imogene, except *sharp* because of her knees and elbows which she used like weapons to leave you black and blue.

But now, suddenly, they all turned out to fit. Imogene *was* cunning and shrewd. She *was* inventive. Nobody else thought of buttering

Boyd's head or washing their cat at the Laundromat. She was creative, if you count drawing pictures on Howard . . . and enterprising, if you count charging money to look at him. She was also powerful enough to keep everybody away from the teachers' room forever, and human enough to give Howard her blanket.

Imogene *was* all the things I said she was, and more, and they were good things to be—depending on who it was doing the inventing or the creating or the enterprising. If Imogene could keep it up, I thought, till she got to be civilized, if that ever happened, she could be almost anything she wanted to be in life.

She could be Imogene Herdman, President . . . or, of course, Imogene Herdman, Jailbird. It would be up to her.

At the end of the day Miss Kemp said, "Which was harder—to give compliments or to receive them?" and everyone agreed that it was really uncomfortable to have somebody tell you, in public, about the best hidden parts of you. Alice, however, made this long, big-word speech about how it was harder for her to *give* compliments because she wanted to be very accurate and truthful, "and not make things up," she said, looking at me.

"I didn't make things up," I told her later, "except, maybe, brave. I don't know whether Imogene is brave."

"You made her sound like some wonderful person," Alice said, "and if that's not making things up, what is?"

When the bell rang everybody whooped out to get started on summer, but Imogene grabbed me in the hall, shoved a Magic Marker in my face, and told me to write the words on her arm.

"On your arm?" I said.

"That's where I keep notes," she said, and I could believe it because I could still see the remains of several messages—something pizza . . . big rat . . . get Gladys . . .

Get Gladys something? I wondered. No, probably just get Gladys.

There was only room for one word on her skinny arm, so Imogene picked *resourceful.* "It's the best one," she said. "I looked it up and I like it. It's way better than graceful, no offense." She turned her arm around, admiring the word. "I like it a lot. I'm gonna get it tattooed."

I didn't ask who by—Gladys, probably.

Charlie was waiting for me on the corner, looking gloomy. He always looks gloomy on the last day of school, and it's always for the same reason.

"It happened again," he said. "Leroy Herdman didn't get kept back."

"Leroy Herdman will never be kept back," I told him. "None of them will."

"He's going to be in my room forever!" he groaned. "What am I going to do?"

"Charlie," I said, "you're going to have to learn to be . . . resourceful."

"How?" he said. "What is it?"

"Ask Imogene," I said. "I think it's going to be her best thing."

Read more about the Herdmans in

The Best Halloween Ever

It was the principal's idea, but it was the Herdmans' fault, according to my mother.

"Don't blame Mr. Crabtree," she said. "It wasn't Mr. Crabtree who piled eight kids into the revolving door at the bank. It wasn't Mr. Crabtree who put the guppies on the pizza. It was one of the Herdmans, or some of the Herdmans, or all of the Herdmans . . . so if there's no Halloween this year, it's their fault!"

Of course the Herdmans couldn't cancel

Halloween everywhere. That's what I told my little brother, Charlie. Charlie kept saying, "I can't believe this!"—as if it was unusual for the Herdmans to mess things up for everybody else.

It wasn't unusual. There were six Herdmans—Ralph, Imogene, Leroy, Claude, Ollie, and Gladys—plus their crazy cat, which was missing one eye and half its tail and most of its fur and any good nature it ever had. It bit the mailman and it bit the Avon lady, and after that it had to be kept on a chain, which is what most people wanted to do with the Herdmans.

I used to wonder why their mother didn't do that with them, but, after all, there were six of them and only one of her. She didn't hang around the house much anyway, and you couldn't really blame her—even my mother said you couldn't really blame her.

They lived over a garage at the bottom of

Sproul Hill and their yard was full of what-ever used to be in the garage—old tires and rusty tools and broken-down bicycles and the trunk of a car (no car, just the trunk)—and I guess the neighbors would have complained about the mess except that all the neighbors had moved somewhere else.

"Lucky for them!" Charlie grumbled. "They don't have to go to school with Leroy like I do."

Like we all do, actually. The Herdmans were spread out through Woodrow Wilson School, one to each grade, and I guess if there had been any more of them they would have wiped out the school and everybody in it.

As it was they'd wiped out Flag Day when they stole the flag, and Arbor Day when they stole the tree. They had ruined fire drills and school assemblies and PTA bake sales, and they let all the kindergarten mice out of their cage and then filled up the cage with guinea pigs.

The whole kindergarten got hysterical about this. Some kids thought the guinea pigs ate their mice. Some kids thought the guinea pigs *were* their mice, grown gigantic overnight. They were all scared and sobbing and hiccuping, and the janitor had to come and remove the guinea pigs.

All the mice got away, so I guess if you were a mouse you would be crazy about the Herdmans. I don't know whether mice get together and one of them says, "How was your day?"—but if that happens, these mice would say, "Terrific!"

"So was that it, Beth?" Charlie asked me. "The mice and the guinea pigs? Was that, like, the last straw, and then everybody said, 'All right, that's it, the last straw . . . no Halloween'? Was that it?"

"I don't think so," I said. "I think it was everything else."

There had been a lot of everything else

because Labor Day was late, so school started late. Parents had an extra week to buy their kids school shoes and get their hair cut; kids had an extra week to finish the fort or tree house or bike trail or whatever else they'd been building since June; and teachers had an extra week to pray they wouldn't have any Herdmans, I guess. . . . And of course the Herdmans had an extra week, too, to tear up whatever they'd missed during the summer.

That turned out to be a lot and, as usual with the Herdmans, it wasn't always things you would *expect* them to do.

The police guard at the bank said that he had seen them come in. "Can't miss *them*!" he said. "So I went right over and stood by the big fish tank. I figure, if I see a bank robber coming I'll defend the money, but if I see those kids coming I'll defend the fish." He shook his head and sighed. "Didn't occur to me to hang around the revolving door."

Nobody got hurt and everybody got out all right, but they had to call the fire department to take the door apart, and they had to close the bank till they got the door back up.

The fire chief said he never saw anything like it. "Two kids," he said, "maybe even three kids might go in that door at the same time to see what would happen, but this was eight kids! What you had was one section of a revolving door full of kids. Couldn't move the door forward, couldn't move it back, had to take it down . . . unless, well, you couldn't just leave them in there."

This was supposed to be a joke, but most people thought it would have been a great opportunity to shut the Herdmans up *somewhere*, even in a revolving door.

It *would* have been a great opportunity, except that by then it wasn't Herdmans in the door. It was eight different kids, including Charlie.

"Why?" my father asked him. "Why would you follow the Herdmans anywhere, let alone into a revolving door?"

Charlie shrugged and looked up at the ceiling and down at the floor and finally said he didn't know. "It was just that they were all around," he went on. "There were Herdmans in front of us and Herdmans in back of us, and then Ralph said, 'Let's see how many kids will fit in the door,' and so . . . " He shrugged again.

The bank manager was mad because of his door, and the bank guard was mad because he picked the wrong thing to guard, but nobody blamed him. How could he know what the Herdmans were going to do? Most of the time, I don't think even the Herdmans knew what they were going to do.

I don't think they *planned* to mix up the mice and the guinea pigs until they happened to see some guinea pigs, and I don't think they decided to find some kids and shove them into a revolving door until they happened to see the door and a bunch of kids all at the same place at the same time.

There probably wouldn't have been any trouble at the pizza parlor either if Mr. Santoro hadn't introduced a new variety— sardine pizza—and *that* wouldn't have caused any trouble if Boomer Malone didn't have to get rid of his guppies.

Boomer started out with two guppies in a fishbowl, and by the next week he had about a hundred guppies in jars and bottles and bowls. Mrs. Malone told my mother that she even found guppies in ice cube trays.

Boomer's original idea had been to sell the guppies, but he finally had to pay Leroy Herdman fifty cents to take them away. According to Gladys, they were going to dump all the guppies into their bathtub and then charge kids a quarter to come and see the guppies go down the drain, all at once.

"It won't hurt them," Gladys said. "They'll just go wherever the water goes and swim around. They'll like it."

Maybe so, but it never happened. Before they got the guppies home to the bathtub, Leroy and Claude and Gladys stopped in the pizza parlor, saw six sardine pizzas on the counter, and immediately swapped guppies for the sardines.

Nobody ever did think that sardine pizza would be a success but, as Mr. Santoro said, "After *that*, sardine pizza didn't have a chance."

The Best Christmas Pageant Ever

Hc 0-06-025043-7
Pb 0-06-440275-4
Pb rack 0-06-447044-X
Au 1-559-94497-8

Everyone knows the Herdmans may just be the worst kids in the history of the world—they lie, they steal, they smoke cigars. Still, no one is prepared when they invade church one Sunday—and decide to take over the annual Christmas pageant! None of the Herdmans ever heard the Christmas story before, and their interpretation has a lot of people up in arms. But the actual pageant is full of surprises for everyone, starting with the Herdmans themselves.

"Outrageous, lively, funny and wonderful."

—Denver Post

HarperTrophy®
An Imprint of HarperCollinsPublishers

HarperCollins*Children'sBooks*
www.harperchildrens.com

HarperChildren's Audio

My Brother Louis Measures Worms

Pb 0-06-076672-7

How is it that Louis has been driving his mother's car around town if he's only eight years old? Where did the cat go to have her kittens? Who won the free wedding? Whether it's costume parades, mysterious paint allergies, or bicycle disasters, there's never a dull moment when the Lawson family is around! With all the humor of *The Best Christmas Pageant Ever*, these hilarious stories by Barbara Robinson are sure to please.

"Will leave readers in stitches."　　　—ALA *Booklist*

■ HarperTrophy®
An Imprint of HarperCollinsPublishers

www.harperchildrens.com

■ HarperCollins*Children'sBooks*